FREIGHTER'S WAY

FREIGHTER'S WAY

by

Abe Dancer

Dales Large Print Books
Long Preston, North Yorkshire,
BD23 4ND, England.

British Library Cataloguing in Publication Data.

Dancer, Abe
    Freighter's way.

    A catalogue record of this book is
    available from the British Library

    ISBN   978-1-84262-560-6 pbk

First published in Great Britain in 2006 by Robert Hale Limited

Published in Large Print 2007 by arrangement with
Robert Hale Ltd.

Dales Large Print is an imprint of Library Magna Books Ltd.

Printed and bound in Great Britain by
T.J. (International) Ltd., Cornwall, PL28 8RW

1

THE WORKLOAD

It was the hour when late sun glowed across the flat grasslands. But by the time Jack Harrow had his chestnut gelding settled in its regular stall at the livery barn, the smokiness of first dark was settling over the town. Along a shale path, edged by dusty cottonwoods, he made his way towards the blocky shape of the McRae Boarding-house. He was bone-deep tired, badly needed a meal and four or five hours' sleep. At daybreak the following morning, aboard the supply coach, he'd be rolling out to the mining regions, west of Laurin Flats.

The fading light tempered the weariness of Jack's sunburned face, merged greying temples with his long, dark hair. A sliver of pale scar tissue ran tight beneath his left eye. He wasn't young, but he wasn't old either. He was just a man who'd burdened himself with too much work, lost some verve in doing it. Of late, he'd questioned his intent, his taking leave of a family business. Long before he'd died, Jack's father had said that in ten years, the Harrow family had cut enough posts and pickets to corral the whole of west Montana. Right now, there was little satisfaction or cheer in providing split timber for settlers along the Yellowstone *and* riding shotgun for Rawlins Haulage.

Inside the boarding-house, the lamps of the dining-room were already lit, less than half the tables were occupied. As Jack stood in the swagged doorway leading off the lobby, a man who was eating alone glanced up. He nodded a brief greeting and Jack moved forward, threaded his way among the other tables.

'Evenin',' Jack said.

Ralph Rawlins had his mouth full. With a fork, he indicated the chair opposite him. Jack sat down carefully, dropped his hat to the floor and loosened his gunbelt. Then he settled back and waited for Rawlins to speak.

Rawlins was a spare man, someone who looked like he'd never got comfortable or secure enough to fill out. He made a loud sucking noise, reached for his coffee cup while glancing at Jack.

'You all set for the mornin'?'

'I usually am,' Jack replied with no obvious concern.

'Yeah, well ... I hope you are,' Rawlins agreed, but with a touch of uncertainty.

Jack knew how the man's nervous manner matched the value of the strong box that was bound for Fishtrap and the Leesburg Mine.

'Somethin' I should know ... should be worryin' about? We got somethin' more'n usual to deliver?'

Rawlins gave him a cool look. 'No, it ain't that. An' your worryin's finished when you step down from the box at the end of a run. You ain't saddled with somethin' permanent ... day an' night.'

Jack shook his head slowly. 'I'll try an' forget you said that, Ralph,' he said, with a peck of irritation. 'It's my job to see the payrolls get through, an' up to now I've always done just that. An' while we're on the subject o' bein' saddled with somethin', you think you'd be here now if your pa had got himself stewed about every one of his coaches an' wagons that rolled towards the Beaverheads?'

Rawlins sniffed, his eyes shifting around. 'I didn't ask for no goddamn sermon. Just drop it.'

'It was you picked it up, sort of implied I

9

ain't conscientious,' Jack retorted. He turned to consider his order as a chubby waitress placed a water glass and cutlery in front of him.

'One day I'm takin' you away from all this,' he said, and smiled at her. 'Or is it you takin' me?'

'That'll be more likely,' she answered sadly. 'I got your favourite chicken pieces saved. There's some fancy tinned fruit … cream, too. Must be borderin' on a feller's heart.'

There was an indifferent silence while Rawlins finished off his meal. When he rose from the table he shoved a paltry tip beneath his plate. For a moment he hesitated, looked at Harrow as though he had something more to say. But then he took a narrow-brimmed derby from a peg on the wall, turned away and went for the door.

'Find yourself a good woman. Don't get off beam all your life,' Jack called out, as Rawlins stepped out on to the walkway.

Jack winked at the waitress as she brought him his food. As he ate, he considered the relationship, the similarities and differences between him and his employer. Ralph Rawlins was the weak progeny of a hard-fisted, stage-line builder. Like Jack, Ralph's father had died leaving a business that his son didn't want or care for. But that's where the similarities ended. Unlike Jack, Ralph was faint-hearted and incompetent.

Jack finished eating. He wiped his chin and looked for the waitress, wondered how grateful she'd be for a little more of his attention. But he thought better of it, and her. He paid, left a more than decent gratuity and stood outside to build himself a smoke. It was turning into a crisp night, a thin band of red sky still pressed upon the dark outline of the Beaverhead Mountains. He glanced at the steps that led up to his room, his home for the nights he stayed in Laurin Flats.

A pie buggy turned along the street towards him, its sturdy wheels hardly raising the dust. He stood and watched while the team pulled over, touched his hat at the small figure that held the reins.

'Nell,' he acknowledged simply, and nodded at the passenger. 'How are you, Craw?'

'Still got me a cough an' a spit.' Crawford Menroe returned Jack's greeting, but his voice lacked warmth.

'We just came from Humble's. He had an order of yours ... somethin' that came in on

11

the bull train,' Nell said quickly, and as an obvious counter to Menroe's response.

Jack thought for a moment, then held up his hand. 'That'll be them bales o' horse barb I've been waitin' for. I'll pick 'em up tomorrow, when I get back from the run.'

'We've got stores for the ranch, so we can haul it for you. Actually, it's already on board.'

'Well, thanks, Nell, that's real neighbourly,' Jack rubbed. 'That kind o' wire's a mighty unpleasant load. My place ain't exactly in your way, neither.'

'Don't tell me you ain't acceptin' offers from a friendly neighbour, Jack. You want we should off-load here in the street?'

Jack sensed the change in her voice, as if she'd wanted him to turn down her offer. It was her way, looking for an excuse to kindle him. It was a regular source of bafflement to Jack. As he shuffled the words of his reply, Menroe shifted on the wagon seat.

'O' course he don't,' the man rumbled irritably. 'An' as you're set to ride us out of our way, we'd best get moving; it's a far piece.'

Nell nodded and lifted the reins. She gave Jack a brief look, a careless, 'Good night.'

A moment later the leathers snapped and

stung at the rumps of the mules. Jack stood watching the buggy draw away into the darkness, saw his two bales of wire that strained the rear axle.

He took a last draw on his cigarette, flicked away the scrawny stub. He realized he should have thanked Nell Yuman straight off, not made a meal about her wanting to help him out. It wasn't as if he didn't have regard for her. And she meant well, like most of the townsfolk, knew he was hard-pressed and all. He swore to himself, put it all down to his tiredness and hoped she'd understand.

Full dark descended on the town and Jack stepped back into the lobby. He heard the clatter of plates as he lifted his key from the register board. 'Goodnight, Precious,' he said towards the kitchen, but not so's the girl would hear. Outside again, he looked into the night, then climbed the narrow staircase to his quarters.

2

PROPOSITIONED

Jack knew the room well enough, had no need of a lamp to find his way around. Not even to avoid tripping on the frayed carpet that was nailed to the boards in front of the wash stand. He ran the window open and stood a moment to let in the westerly night breeze. Then he edged to the mattress, rolled his fist into the unyielding wad. The boarding-house was owned by the girl's ma – the original and legendary warden who took a bite if she found you still abed at the crack of dawn. Jack raised a thin smile at the thought of there being no working locks on any of the rooms. From somewhere below, there was a rattling crash followed by a shrill curse. It was Precious, and Jack pondered on how unlucky you could get.

He wasn't long into restless sleep, when a close-by knocking brought him fully awake. He rolled on to his side, his fingers reaching under the cot frame for his gunbelt.

'Who is it? What's up?' he called.

There was no response, just another short rat-a-tap from the other side of the door.

'Wait up an' shut up,' Jack rasped. He reached for the room's table, touched the lamp and struck a match. He swore at the flare of brightness, but it stung his reflexes as he padded long-johned and barefoot across the boards. He pulled open the door and thrust the barrel of his Colt into a dark silhouette. 'Night-soil's below,' he said, short and tetchily.

The man was big and he almost smiled. 'Huh, I was told there was a way about you – if you're Jack Harrow, that is,' he said unhurriedly.

Jack lowered the gun barrel, but he was cross from being awakened. 'I'm him, an' *you* better have some explanation for rousin' me, mister, else you'll see I got a *real scary* way.'

'My name's Ormer Pugg, an' I'm sorry to come disturbin' you,' the man quickly declared. 'I fingered your room 'cause I know'd you be pullin' out early mornin'. If you'll just let me talk for a bit, I won't be usin' up much time.'

'Come in, an' this better be good ... or interestin',' Jack told him.

Jack closed the window. He'd forgotten about night temperatures on the weather side of the Beaverheads. 'Get on with it,' he said.

The man entered the room as far as the weak lamplight showed his broad face and his close-cropped fair hair. 'I've got a proposition for you,' he started. 'The few days I've been in town, I've done some askin'. Thought I might o' heard o' you before, but I guess *that* feller wouldn'ta been makin' fences for a livin'. Local word is, you're reliable, ain't afraid o' hard graft, an' as honest as...' Pugg stopped and grinned. 'Well, two out o' three's good enough for what I want,' he added.

Jack let his gun hand drop, wondered if he'd have to get dressed, if there'd be any more sleep for him that night. 'That's your proposition?' he asked. 'With all that righteous stuff, you want me to run for mayor, corner preach on the sabbath?'

The man's teeth flashed in a more open smile. 'I heard you took over from your folk to get 'em out o' trouble. But that was a while back, and you still ain't removed yourself from a shirt-tail business. Ain't that why you're shotgun messenger for Ralph Rawlins?'

'Shirt-tail maybe, Mr Ormer Pugg, but it's mine. Go careful.' Jack looked impassive, but a nerve flicked at the edge of the scar on his face.

'I'll pay you twice what you're gettin' from Rawlins. Same work, 'cept for me,' Pugg continued more abruptly.

'You got me discomfited ... don't normally parley with me drawers around me ankles,' Jack said. 'But I'm a tad interested. Like, how the hell you goin' to find enough o' the same work out o' Laurin Flats. Rawlins' crates ain't exactly fit to bust.'

Pugg nodded. 'I understand, but as I'm doin' the payin', that'll be my concern, not yours, or anyone else's. If you're interested, you can start right off ... make whatever arrangements you have to, o' course. First light for first shipment? What d'you say?'

'I'd say I ain't too interested in sellin' out Ralph Rawlins. After all, I'm straight. You said so yourself, or were about to.'

Pugg held out his hands, spoke with a little more animation. 'For God's sake, Harrow, you know as well as I do, that sort o' heavy carryin's done for. An' there ain't enough folk that needs small doin's, anymore. Them that do, collects it from the freight head at Butte. Them Rawlinses can't last much longer an' you know it. None o' you small-timers can. Your businesses are dead.' Pugg made the cut-throat sign, looked for Jack's acknowledgment.

Jack's response was to take a threatening step towards the big man. 'Your manner's wearin' a bit thin, so's my patience, an' I'm already bushed. Now, I ain't seen or heard anythin' yet that I like about you, Pugg, so you leavin' peaceable or otherwise?'

Pugg cocked his head to one side. He was thinking of the way through, the next ploy. A foxy smile creased his broad face and he took a small step back.

'I been overlookin' somethin' here,' he said. 'It's just got to be Rawlins' sister. Hear tell she's a piece o' candy, got ten times the looks an' grit o' that weak-kneed brother of hers. There's some say, she'll give you a better ride than that old mud wagon you call a–'

Jack hit him then. It was hardly without warning. If Pugg didn't know it, he should have. In one movement, Jack dropped his Colt, with his fist smashed the man's unfinished words back into his mouth. There was some timing and anger in the blow, and Pugg's head snapped back, moved the solid neck, then the rest of the body. With a low grunt, Pugg dropped his hands that groped for support. The chair beside the door trapped the man's faltering legs and he went down. His weight cracked the seat and broke the back apart, the noise beating around the room.

Jack winced at the pain across his knuckles, sucked air through his teeth. 'Now you got me fully woke,' he said. 'An' most others in these parts.'

Pugg was dragging a leg, trying to force his way back up. The lower half of his face had already started to swell, and angry colour was framing incensed, hard eyes. Blood started to ooze around his chin as, now on his knees, he lifted his right hand toward his left armpit.

Pugg's dark coat fell away, but he didn't touch the gun that was holstered there. Instead he reached for his hat and drew himself slowly to his feet. He turned away from the light, hiding the emotion in his eyes. 'You sure hit hard, friend,' he slurred thickly. 'Musta played my hand all wrong.'

Without taking his eyes off Pugg, Jack stooped to pick up his Colt. He drew back the hammer as Pugg fell against the door before wrenching it open.

'You made a mistake tonight,' Jack said coldly.

'You showed me a weakness: maybe that was *your* mistake.' Pugg coughed, stepped onto the platform at the top of the stairs. He paused for a moment, then made his way determinedly down to the street.

Jack stepped to the door and kicked it closed. He leaned his back against it, stayed that way for a long moment. Rachel Rawlins, he thought. 'Gave myself away there,' he said jadedly. 'I wonder what the night caller's goin' to do about it.'

3

THE SHIPMENT

Rachel Rawlins looked up when Jack came into the haulage office. 'Hello, Jack,' she said, with a friendly smile. 'You've opened up a fine day.'

A whiskey drummer and a stock buyer were sitting on the bench alongside the door waiting for the Fishtrap stage. They paid no heed to Jack, their interest fixed boorishly on the girl at her desk. Jack nodded to them briefly, placed his hat on one of the filing cupboards that divided the offices.

'Funny, ain't it, how some folk can have an opinion without knowin' the facts?' he answered without looking up. He went to a rack fastened to the rear wall of the office and picked out two pieces from the short order of firearms. He looked briefly at the mechanisms, the shiny, oiled barrels. Then he took some shells, loaded both guns and tipped the rest into his coat pocket.

The girl pushed her chair away from her

desk, stood up and walked towards him casually. 'Just as funny,' she retorted, 'the way some folk leave their good humour in the can. Only of course, it really ain't funny.'

Jack took a sharp look at her as he shoved his hat back on his head. 'Where's your brother?' he asked. He wasn't in the best of moods for good reason, thought it advisable not to continue the banter.

'Where he usually is at this hour ... at the stable gettin' the team hitched. Meeling's with Mr Treebucks at the bank collectin' the payroll. We're all on schedule, Jack,' Rachel remarked, her satisfaction obvious.

'That's all you need to do,' he said. 'Most folk need an' want reliability. That's what they pay for. Stay with it, an' you'll keep everyone's noses above water.'

A frown touched Rachel's brow. 'Do you mean somethin' by that?' she asked.

'Yeah, guess I do,' Jack said, and told her about his visitor of the night before, of Ormer Pugg's intent, his offer. As he talked, he caught a new expression on Rachel's face. It was a more serious one, and touched by worry.

'Well it ain't goin' to be pound for pound competition he's after,' she affirmed. 'So I guess it must be *us* ... somethin' personal.

Perhaps Ralph knows what's goin' on. If there's to be cut-throat dealin', maybe it'll raise his dander. But whatever it is, we've little to fear with *you* decidin' to hitch with Rawlins Haulage, eh, Jack?' Rachel reached out and gave Jack's upper arm muscle a teasing squeeze.

Jack doubted if Ralph knew what was going on with Pugg. Rachel's brother certainly had something on his mind, but Jack doubted it was concern over a rival operator. But before he had a chance to discuss it any more, they all heard the coach rolling up from the stable yard.

Stifling a derisive laugh, Jack turned away. 'Yeah, you could ask Ralph,' he said. 'Be careful though. Late yesterday, he looked like he was goin' short on the trigger.' Gripping a shotgun, Jack told the two seated business-men to make ready, then he went out to the boardwalk.

The early morning sun slanted into the street, sparkled the rising dust motes around the hoofs of the team. In its heyday, the coach had been a handsome one. But Montana's scorching sun, scouring sand and winter snow had long since wreaked its worst. Fancy scrollwork and bright paint were now lost to bleached and cracked panelling. But the vehicle was sturdy, well made for endurance and it ran true.

Jack stepped around to the front near-side of the ageing vehicle, offered up his brace of guns to Harvey Maud, the driver. Then he made a smoke, watched thoughtfully, as downstreet, two men approached from the direction of the bank. Between them, they carried the payroll shipment for the workers of the Leesburg Mine. It was a heavy, iron-bound box that represented Jack's safekeeping and commitment.

The mining company's local manager was Owen Treebucks, a man whose shrewdness didn't go much beyond having the good sense to stay reserved and unnoticed.

Jack made a curt greeting and looked at the second man. 'Thanks, but I can probably manage without you,' he said with a thin smile and unnoticed sarcasm.

Parker Meeling was the Rawlins' clerk, an uninteresting, unfriendly and unhelpful man who hardly bothered to clear a sentence with anyone. Jack relieved him of the express box, swore as he heaved it up the side of the coach. 'No, sir, help's an almighty overrated service,' he muttered for the umpteenth time in six months.

The two passengers had got themselves

seated inside the big coach. Maud had finished stowing their assortment of carpetbags and cases in the rear boot, had buckled up the broad straps. He stuffed the waybill that Rachel Rawlins had given him into a shirt pocket and climbed up to his seat. Jack settled beside him, resigned himself to the smell of horse-sweat and dust, to the long and weary miles ahead of them.

Maud lifted his whip from its pocket, and to the crack of a rawhide popper, the horses surged into their collars. A shattering whoop broke from Maud's throat, and the heavy-set coach rolled forward.

Jack turned to look back. He raised a farewell hand to Rachel who was watching from the office's doorway. She waved in return, stood for a moment, as the dust swirled and eddied along the street.

As the coach turned past McRae's, Jack sighted the hefty figure Ormer Pugg. He stood leaning against an upright at a corner of the building. His aching head turned stiffly with his body as he watched the coach roll by. His deep-set eyes presaged a grudge, posted a reprisal out to Jack.

Ten minutes later, the straggling outbuildings of Laurin Flats faded away, and the road started to snake through ochred stretches of sage and bunch grass. They were headed west toward the Leesburg mines, the timbered hills of Beaverhead Mountains.

Jack tugged at the brim of his hat, squinted against the slip of wind. He pushed the guard guns deep into their boot holsters, shifted and wriggled for a more comfortable position. For a short time his thoughts turned to Rachel Rawlins, then intriguingly on to Precious McRae. Rachel would be the girl to provide feist and fascination. But Jack wagered it would be Precious who'd shape him a sumptuous seat cushion.

An hour passed and the horses settled further into their collars. They were climbing steadily now, up and away from the flat rangeland. Ridges of timber rose about them, and rocks were scattered among the spruce and juniper. Jack's humour had improved, and, lulled by the rock and roll of the coach, he dozed a little, nodded quietly beside Harvey Maud.

More miles and, for a few more, the road topped out onto a narrow benchland with the timberline still ahead of them. Then they were climbing again, with heavier timber pressing in, tall thick-boled yellow pine that dibbed the gigantic sky.

Harvey Maud knew just how much he

could demand from his five-horse spike. When the rear pair tired, risked breaking their stride, he hauled in for the first breather. It was a cold-harbour rest, but timely, before their route would take them sharply upward through a narrow, rocky draw.

4

ROAD AGENTS

Kicking at the brake lever, Maud leaned out and yelled down to the passengers, 'Stretch your legs, gents ... take a leak ... anythin' you can get done in ten minutes.'

As the coach still rocked on its thorough-braces the doors banged open. Glad of the break, both passengers extricated themselves stiffly.

Jack hitched a leg over the seat rail. He was easing his weight for the swing down when, from the trees hard to the roadside, the masked men stepped out. He groaned, cursed, realized they'd waited for just that moment. He nearly smiled at his vulner-ability.

The men were dressed in spent range garb, but their guns gleamed, looked well cared for. One of the two men was levelling a Colt, the other had a saddle gun aimed at Jack's middle. From under the red and white chequered cloth that covered most of his face, he said sharply, 'Just stay hangin', Mr Shotgun. Anyone else got a mind for collectin' lead … make a move.'

A startled squawk broke from the whiskey drummer, but that was all. No one was offering resistance against the drawn guns. At an order from the second hold-up man, the passengers lifted their arms and lined up beside the coach. The man stepped close and fanned them for weapons, but only the stock buyer was armed. The tall, pale-featured man snorted at the small-bore pistol before lobbing it into the scrub. 'Best place for it,' he said in a throaty voice, and stepped away.

The man with the saddle gun hadn't taken his attention from the two men on the driver's seat. Maud had been caught there too, but he was reasonably assured of a pension pay-out from the Rawlins company and wasn't going to jeopardize it.

'Now you, Ribbon Man, take the gun from your guard's holster and drop it down here,' the man ordered him. 'Be real careful. Use your left hand. You both look clever enough to know what happens if you go for bravery.'

Maud had no choice. His face was puffed, flushed with anger. He did as he was told and took Jack's Colt, tossed it down towards the man's feet. Then the carbine barrel jerked, indicated that he move back to his driver's position.

Jack had hardly moved since the two men had showed from the trees. But he'd thought out the movements, the options he had in making a play. He looked down at the masked faces, showed no obvious response when a breath of wind caught the edge of the plaid cloth, briefly curled it from the quiet man's face.

'Throw down the box,' the man now said.

Jack made no move. 'Nothin' too brave about tellin' you, this is a big, big mistake,' he advised.

'Yeah, *yours* if you don't get it down here,' the man responded, his eyes and voice holding no change. 'An' I can tell the difference from a cash-box an' any old scattergun you mighta got hidden up there.'

For the shortest of moments there was the zing of challenge in the air, and the assembled men sensed it. Then Jack bent to the command and stretched an arm down into the boot.

Maud sucked air between his teeth as Jack moved, but Jack stayed his hand from the gnarled stock of the shotgun. He seized a lifting ring on the side of the cash-box and dragged it up to the seat. The man with the carbine nodded, and Jack turned it up and over the seat rail, watched as it thudded into the packed dirt below.

'It ain't that heavy. Take it back to the horses. I'll come on,' the man told his partner.

The box was all they'd wanted, took no interest in robbing the passengers. The man kicked Jack's Colt further away from the coach, then lifted the box with apparent ease. He straightened, took a quick look at both Jack and Maud before hefting the load back from where he'd come. Jack doubted they'd got themselves a buggy, guessed it was where they'd left a couple of horses.

Harvey Maud was breathing loudly and laboriously. Jack knew he was still wondering about the shotgun, how and why it hadn't got to be used.

'You got robbed, that's all. No one died,' the man with the carbine said, as if in explanation. He didn't say any more, just retreated slowly, but all the while keeping a questioning eye on Jack. He'd almost reached the shadowy barrier of pine, when Maud made his decision.

'Goddamn it,' he exclaimed. 'I ain't goin' to collect any annuity by not puttin' up a fight.' Then, with a grunt he dropped to his knees, seized the shotgun in his gloved hands and jabbed it out towards the retreating hold-up man.

The gun's muzzles cleared the side of the boot and found their target, then connected sharply with the upward sweep of Jack's forearm. The triggers jerked under Maud's hand and both barrels discharged in a roar of sound. A crashing hail of shot went skywards, whipping at the golden-sunned pine tops. The horses were momentarily panicked, they stomped and snorted, and the coach rocked against the set of the brake.

A full minute later, when the echoes of the blast had died away, the sounds of two horses could be clearly heard. The hoofs were clipping at the ground, fast moving in a hasty retreat.

Maud was bewildered. His eyes moved from the still smoking barrels of the shotgun to Jack.

'You'da had him for sure, Harve,' Jack said, quietly. 'I lost my balance there for a bit tryin' to get out o' your way.' Then he twisted away, went down the side of the coach.

'All aboard, gents, excitement's over,' Jack told the anxious businessman. 'Most companies would charge you an extra ten dollars for that kind o' sideshow.'

The businessmen had realized that any further danger was over. Jack waved aside their questions about what had happened. He picked up his gun from the dust and blew at the barrel. 'We all got lucky,' he muttered, spinning the cylinder.

The stock buyer looked unsatisfied with Jack's conduct, but he was smart enough to let it ride and went to retrieve his pocket gun from the brush.

'Let's get out o' here,' Maud rasped down from the driver's seat. 'Get in all o' you, and make it quick.'

The passengers scrambled through the doorway and pulled the door to. Jack clambered up to his own seat. Maud loosed the brake lever and yelled at the horses. Then, and in some surprise, Jack realized the man was turning the stage.

'There's no panic, Harve. We ain't got nothin' to get robbed of anymore,' he said.

At the same time, the whiskey drummer pulled aside the canvas and thrust his head from the window. 'Hey, what's happenin' now? You ain't goin' on to Fishtrap?'

'We ain't got no reason,' Maud shouted back timidly.

'We *paid*, that's a goddamn reason. Swing

round,' the man snapped in righteous anger.

'We're headed back to Laurin Flats,' Maud yelled. 'The sooner the sheriff knows about this, the more chance he's got o' stoppin' them varmints. They'll be disappearin' in the hills with their loot... Rawlins' loot.'

The stock buyer leaned from the other window. 'They'll be in sundown, before the sheriff even gets 'imself saddled up, you goddamn rind-brain,' he yelled. Then he swore some more at the driver because he knew it was to no avail.

5

THE CHASE

Elmer Redland's hard features were expressing very little when he walked into the Rawlins Haulage office, despite it being unusual for any coach, wagon or freighter to come larruping into town with its driver in such a state of high excitement.

Outside, a collection of townsfolk were animatedly discussing the situation, ogling the lathered, near-spent team. Inside, the passengers were expressing their anger, taking out their frustration on a troubled Ralph Rawlins. But Rawlins had more of an immediate concern than the profit losses of two businessmen. The sheriff read the situation, accepted Rawlins' silent appeal for help.

'All right, let's have some order here,' he said firmly. 'Anyone would think you'd run into Crazy Horse. I'm guessin' you didn't.'

Jack Harrow was leaning against the filing cabinets with his arms folded. He'd already replaced the shotgun in the rack, now he stood calmly listening. Maud was scowling, breathing deep, holding quiet. Rachel was there too, her knuckles showing white against the back of her chair as it moved back and forth. Her eyes looked very dark against her skin, didn't stray far from Jack. At his clerking desk, Parker Meeling was poker-faced, the only one unmoved enough to stay seated.

'What's the story, Jack?' Redland asked. 'No need for the "once-upon-a-time" bit.'

Jack pulled off his hat, ran the flat of his hand across the top of his head. 'Well, the meat of it *is*, they caught us cold an' took the cash box.' With a few halting sentences, Jack then filled in a bit more about the hold-up. 'Snappy enough for you?'

The sheriff cut a sharp glance at Ralph Rawlins. 'Is that the way you just heard it'?' he asked.

Rawlins nodded. 'Not the sort o' thing you can get significantly wrong, is it?'

'An' that's the way you saw it, Harve?'

The driver screwed up his jowly face. 'Yeah, 'cept I'da put a little more importance on havin' stared down the barrels o' some wayward cannons.' He glanced at Jack. 'That's one o' the things I ain't forgettin' easy,' he furthered with a likely consideration.

'Hmm,' the sheriff pondered. 'What about them turkeys ... two of 'em you say? Would you know 'em again, if you saw 'em walk by here?'

'I would if they were wavin' their pieces about,' Maud grumbled.

'They were both masked, Sheriff. One was tall ... nothin' about their garb to stand out in this part o' the world,' Jack said, not precise or wholly sincere.

The sheriff fingered his chin. 'Both wore masks an' one of 'em was shorter than the other,' he repeated wryly. 'Shouldn't take long to get 'em behind bars then, should it? Not if you could throw in which way it was they hightailed,' he added.

'There's maybe a rockchuck saw 'em, Sheriff. We only got to hear 'em. But up in them hills, the sounds can fool you ... mash up the pin-pointin'.'

'Then I guess I'll have to drag my old ass up in to the saddle,' Redland grunted. He gave a resigned shrug, speculated on the fast rounding up of a posse.

'I want to know how long we're goin' to be stuck here,' the whiskey drummer stated impatiently. 'I'm losin' money.'

'An' what the hell d'you think I'm losin', mister?' Ralph Rawlins retorted hotly. 'I've already apologized. There'll be a coach leavin' in the mornin': same time, same place.'

'That means I'll have to spend another night in that cow pen you called a hotel.'

Jack was thinking of agreeing with the man, especially about getting a night's sleep, when Maud interrupted.

'Ralph, can I talk to you? It's important,' he said. 'You too, Sheriff. Won't take but a minute.'

The haulage proprietor gestured towards the door of a small room to one side of the main office. 'Yeah, I guess. We'll go in there; it's quieter. An' it looks like you've got somethin' on your mind.'

Rachel moved as though to follow her brother, then for some reason she stopped.

Jack had the inkling of an idea of what was going on, and he nodded non-committally at her, went back out into the afternoon sun. He stood on the front step of the coach, reached up and into the boot. He pulled out the second gun and pushed it into his coat pocket, stepped down again and winked at one of the onlookers. 'Can't be too careful,' he said. 'There's robbers afoot.'

The uneasy feeling returned, nipped at his vitals as he walked away from the haulage office. He quickened his pace, back towards where his chestnut was stabled. As he turned the corner of the bank, he almost collided with Owen Treebucks.

'Hey, I'm goin' to the...' the man started to say. 'Where're *you* goin'? They said there's been a holdup,' he blustered, making a grab for Jack's arm.

Instantly irritated, Jack stepped back. 'Yeah, *they're* right,' he agreed. 'Go ask Rawlins, he's at the office still.'

'The payroll's gone?' demanded the mine operator. His voice was alarmed, as Jack carried on past him. 'You're the company's guard. You can't leave.'

'Watch me,' Jack offered, and kept on going until he made the livery barn.

He swung up the retaining bar, pulled open the double doors and met the heady rush of warm hay and horse odour. His chestnut was in its end stall and Jack worked quickly with the blanket saddle and traps. In less than five minutes he was mounted up, ducking his head to clear the doorway.

Out in the street he saw the advancing group of men, with the sheriff leading them. Some of them would be coming for their mounts, others would be for him. 'Maud,' he grated knowingly.

The lawman raised his arm the moment

he saw Jack. 'Heave to, feller. There's one or two more questions need answerin'.'

Jack squared himself in saddle and kicked with his boot heels, 'Goddamn right,' he swore, as he swerved the gelding, hauled it into a gallop away from the men who were pressing forward excitedly.

He swung west out of the end of town, headed back for the deep shelter of the hills. He knew his horse was fresh. He could push it hard, take a chance on resting later on. After what seemed an age, he glanced back, saw the puff of dust against the lower sky. It meant Redland had a bunch of riders together, was making pursuit. He reined down, and swung off the gelding's back. While it puffed and snatched at cranesbill, he stood and watched the small dust cloud, estimated the posse's rate of travel.

When he was up in the hills, Jack knew he'd lose them. For storekeepers and farmers the running was good, exhilarating even. But there was no charge against him and no reward, so once they'd lost him, there'd be very little incentive, and the sheriff would know it. He gave the cinch a tug and swung into the saddle. 'Let's go,' he said, and the chestnut made a fast clip through the bunch grass, set its head for the shelving hills.

6

THE BEAVERHEADS

Another hour had passed when Jack pulled in to the shadow of a stand of spruce. Dismounting, he listened again, enthralled by the power of silence. Below the ridge he looked back on the ravines of standing timber; beyond that was Laurin Flats and the dusty benches. Somewhere between the two, he was sure, the sheriff and his makeshift posse had lost his trail. If he kept a watchful eye, they'd never get close.

It took him a while to locate the rocky draw; then below it, the stage road, where the robbery had taken place that very morning. Jack thought it likely that the two hold-up men had ridden close to where he stood now. They would have climbed away from the coach, looked for a higher route through the timber. This way, they could have taken their time, run fewer risks of being spotted. They'd wend through the peaks, make tracks down through the string of worked-out mines towards the Idaho border.

Jack took to his saddle again. Hunting constantly for sign, he struck out, swung in a wide, slow circle. It was hard going over the steep, mountainous hills, and the day dragged on, reached late afternoon. If he was caught out by nightfall, he'd feel the chill when the sun dropped behind the high peaks. And with no track to follow, his quarry would get many hours ahead of him, cover too many miles for him to close up. But he reasoned, then hoped he'd cut a trail soon. He wasn't an eager spoor for wolves, cougars, big brown bears; any carnivore in search of its nightly meats.

He was almost past the sign before he saw it in the thin soil; fresh imprints of two horses climbing from a rocky shelf just below him. There was no one else in the hills, and Jack got a fix on the way the riders were headed, the pass they were likely bound for. He lifted the reins, flicked the gelding forward again. He was filling the hole, no more need to get slowed with sign hunting.

Jack was well in to the pass before first dark. The air was thin and cold, some ribbons of unmelted snow still clung to the low shadowed rocks. Through the western end of the pass, the ground sloped away, the sun, a deep red fireball ahead of him. He reined in where long shadows of dusk spread from a clump of aspen, took a few deep breaths and compassed the slag heaps and crumbling structures of the abandoned mine works.

For an hour, Jack watched the wrecked buildings, sluice towers and buckled shaft openings that pocked the barren slopes. But nestled among them was one cabin that hadn't surrendered to the mine's spectres; a yellow square of light glowed from behind one of its dust-caked windows.

The hold-up men would have their horses picketed at graze somewhere in the trees below the overgrown belt of land, but Jack couldn't see them from where he hunkered. The men weren't killers; they'd said as much themselves as they stashed the cash box. So, for one further walk, Jack held the bridle reins loosely and walked the gelding straight at the cabin. He adjusted his gunbelt, but doubted there'd be any need for quick gun play.

He had gone only a few yards when the light in the cabin went out. The gelding's irons were striking and ringing off rock fragments as they approached. But Jack continued impassively until he stood within a dozen feet of the cabin's doorway.

He waited a full minute before the door cracked open. A woody groan, cleaved the dark silence, disguised the voice of the man who wore a chequered neckcloth.

'Mine's closed,' he rasped. 'So's everythin' else up here. What do you want?'

Jack let the bridle reins drop. 'My name's Jack Harrow, an' I ain't a total stranger to these parts,' he said. 'Maybe we should talk.'

'Jack Harrow, eh?' the man reflected. 'Who you brought with you?'

'No one. I thought it best I come alone. You must've known I'd show up.'

'Maybe,' the man said. 'There weren't no must about it, though.' Then he took a half step back into the cabin, exchanged a few words with his partner.

Jack weighed up the situation. Assuming the man came to the door a second time, if something happened he didn't like, he could drop him, take evasive action before the second man got a gun involved. But then a match flared, and the light from inside flickered up again. It shone at the gap of the opening door, the man's shadowy profile as he edged it wider.

The man indicated that Jack step inside. 'You'll be the first to die, if you ain't alone,' he advised, as he moved back.

As it appeared from the outside, the building was a tumbledown wreck. Opposite the door, a green wood fire burned in a cracked, iron stove. To the right, a couple of box bunks were hanging away from the wall. The lower one held the broken open Leesburg Mine payroll box. To the left, cracker crates served as furniture. A clutch of Wanted posters were nailed up, tie-ropes hung from a row of wooden pegs, and tin dishes lay upon a pile of firewood. Hanging low above their heads, the wall of an army squadron tent served as a roof.

'Sure beats the hell out o' livin' rough,' Jack muttered, as the pungent smoke caught the back of his throat.

The man with the neckcloth, placed the barrel of his carbine against the door, shoved it half closed. 'I've known worse,' he replied. 'There's a cat-house this side o' the hogback, got rooms so dirty, there's a sign over the door asks you to clean your boots before takin' to the street.'

Jack gave the man a sideways look and nearly smiled.

The second man in the cabin, stood beside the stove. He was angular tall, carried a long broken nose and his thin hair stuck to his scalp; of a sort that made ordinary folk feel uncomfortable. 'How'd you find this place?' he snarled. 'I knew we shouldn'ta trusted that–'

'Shut it, Gruse,' the other man's voice threatened.

Jack identified the gaffe. 'I followed your tracks up here ... didn't need no help,' he said, straightaway wondered if 'Gruse' was a dub for something else.

'You sure there ain't no one behind you ... like a star-toter from Laurin Flats?'

Jack shook his head. 'I already said, no, an' it weren't my intention. But if I followed you here, then I guess someone else could. It's a possibility you got to consider.'

'Best take a turn out there, Gruse,' the other man put in. 'If you hear anythin', fire off that Colt. If they're that close, it'll be too late to worry, an' they won't be seein' you.'

Gruse hesitated, his eyes bored into his partner with a displeased, argumentative look. 'If I *do* hear anythin',' he started, 'I'll come back an' fillet this smarty aleck.'

'Don't get lost,' Jack said, as the man sidled past him.

7

REUNION

'Always ribbin', eh Jack?' the man said, a moment or two after Gruse had left the cabin.

'How long's it been, Hote? Two years?' was Jack's answer.

'An' the suet.' Hote Stuckley walked over to the bunks, put an elbow on the top, and a boot on the lower frame. His hand felt the saddle-bags that were spread under the sougan. 'You look pared to the bone. That down to hard work, or not eatin'?' he asked of Jack.

'Both.' Jack glanced at the stove, the blistering coffee pot.

'Help yourself,' Stuckley said. 'I'll call Gruse back. Get him to fry you up some bacon.'

Jack didn't respond, picked the least dirty tin mug from a pile. He filled it with heavily brewed coffee, but it was the way he favoured it.

'We been in some scrapes, Jack,' Stuckley recalled. 'Got out of 'em too. But all that seems like a long time ago. Travelled our separate ways, eh?'

'Yeah, up till now. I'm real disappointed you picked my coach to work over.'

'You think I knew that?' Stuckley growled.

'You knew where Maud would rest the team, what time we'd be along ... give or take. Stands to reason you knew who'd be ridin' shotgun.'

'But–'

'But *what*, Hote?' Jack cut in. 'I shouldn't been there, 'cause Ormer Pugg bought me off? Is that it?'

'Who's Ormer Pugg?' Stuckley asked, his face expressionless, hard for Jack to read.

Jack grinned without humour, started to build himself a cigarette. 'So, one way or another, you musta been real surprised meetin' me out there this mornin'. Nearly as much as I was. Not too surprised to ride on though. Or maybe it was your partner ... ol' angel features ... holdin' you to somethin'.' Jack ignited a match against the sole of his boot.

Stuckley squared up. 'You really got to start watchin' that tongue o' yours, Jack. Would you've taken me out with that goddamn scattergun? Would you, Jack?' he asked suddenly. 'You'd seen my face ... knew it was me.'

Jack shook his head. 'The driver was tryin' to make a name for himself ... grubstake even. He ain't totally stupid neither. I knocked his arm, spoilt his aim, an' he knows it. He told the sheriff as much. That's the reason I'm up here in this hell-hole tonight ... nothin' else, Hote.'

Stuckley considered Jack's story, until the penny dropped. Jack had certainly saved his life, but now he'd come for the money to clear his name. 'Whatever it is your life's full of, Jack, it's a fool's game,' he said, the scowl easing from his face. 'You burnin' up, to make ends meet. Christ, you'll be dead before you get to sit your stoop. Now, if you had a share in this.' Stuckley turned back the sougan, patted a bulging saddle-bag. 'An' there could be plenty more, Jack. Sidin' with me an' Gruse, could be the best thing to happen to you since ... well, since the last time you had a best thing happen.'

Jack gave a rueful shake of his head. 'Yeah, well that was a while ago. But I've got me a campaign, Hote. Reckon I'll ride it out. Means, I got to stay easy side o' the law.'

'Yeah, your joshin's real legendary, Jack. It's the stuff o' music halls. You really think I'm goin' to let you take these dust bags back to town, just so's you can stay sweet with the law? Sorry, partner.'

Jack squinted, moved his head back from the curl of cigarette smoke. Casually he put his gun hand in his coat pocket, moved the flap aside for Stuckley to see the butt of his holstered Colt. 'I just got through tellin' you, Hote,' he said. 'I ain't your partner, not any more.' He pulled the gun as he finished speaking.

With Jack's Colt in his view, the ploy caught Stuckley unawares. The man stared hard at Jack's face for a moment. 'Neat trick, Jack,' he said. 'But if you was goin' to shoot me, you'da done it earlier. Or've let someone else do it.'

'I don't aim to kill you, Hote. I'll break you open a bit ... bust some bones. Imagine holdin' up from a goddamn bath chair. Now, I'll have the luggage.'

Stuckley grinned, wickedly. 'Remember, all them that say g'night ain't necessarily goin' home.' But there was no softening of Jack's line, so he shrugged, dragged at the saddle-bags and swung them down at Jack's feet.

Jack nodded. 'You try an' follow me, Hote, an' you certainly won't be goin' home ... wherever that is. Now get your face stuck into that cot.'

Without further protest, Stuckley stretched out on the lower bunk. Jack stepped forward and lifted the man's gun from his belt, tossed it into the pile of firewood. He pulled one of the short lengths of rope from its peg, fashioned a loop.

Jack wasn't sure of Gruse's resolve, whether or not he'd think it safer back in the cabin, so now he worked fast. He threw a couple of bowknots around Stuckley's wrists, and the man swore. Jack told him to shut up. 'You're lucky I ain't usin' barbwire,' he said. He was going to plug Stuckley's mouth with the chequered neckcloth, but realized it was a needless precaution.

'This should keep you occupied for a while,' he said, straightening up. 'But I'd sure try an' work your way out before that ugly son-of-a-bitch gets back.'

'Why?' Stuckley asked, as he moved his tied-up hands into the small of his back.

'Because I'm goddamn sure he ain't gettin' any jump from a woman. An' with you trussed up an' all...' Jack, picked up the saddle-bags, swung them across a shoulder. 'But that's *your* problem: I got what I came for,' he said, distractedly.

'You started to wonder what to tell the

sheriff, Jack?' Stuckley asked of him.

'I'll think o' somethin',' Jack replied, dragging at the door.

Stuckley leaned his head over the edge of the bunk, spat loudly at the dirt-packed ground. 'Yeah, I'm sure you will. You an' me mustn't leave it so long 'til next time,' he said.

Outside, the gelding had stayed on trailing reins. Jack flung the leather pouches up behind the cantle and swung in to the saddle.

Somewhere above him on the torn slopes above the ramshackle mine sheds, Gruse would be keeping watch, but Jack didn't look for him. He walked his horse to the old pack-mule trail and sent it forward. In the open, under the bright starlight, he expected to hear the lookout's challenge, maybe take a back-shot. 'No,' he murmured, knowing that Gruse would be more concerned with a surprise attack from the sheriff's posse, than Jack Harrow's leaving.

8

THE LAW

At the foot of the trail, Jack reined in to the trees and sat for a while. He waited for sounds to wind down from above, but heard nothing. He pushed on again, through a ravine that slanted steep, between hill spurs that were still thick with timber.

The night was getting some age on it, and there would be no moon until maybe an hour before daybreak. There was nothing blacker than the hills of the Beaverheads, with tall, solid pine blanking out the stars. But Jack went on, ever downward, letting the gelding feel its way.

It was a half-hour past midnight when he happened upon a working trail. It bent around the base of a big, rocky spur, was a silvery ribbon he knew to be the coach road that led west to Fishtrap. Jack was familiar with every twist and turn of it, and very shortly got himself sited.

The gelding was tired, but Jack was settled

on pushing forward. He turned east, back to Laurin Flats. If there was a posse out for him, the quicker he could turn the money over to the sheriff the better it would be for him. He took to the road, but now ever mindful of his mount's need for more rest.

It was during a short breather that Jack heard the unmistakable blunt pounding of hoofs. He placed the sound somewhere below and behind him, and headed his way. Under his breath, he swore, heeled the gelding up the shallow bank into the deep, dark shadow of a blue spruce.

Jack's immediate thought was for the two men back at the deserted mine. He was astounded that they would, or even could have, trailed him to recapture the packs full of cash. But whoever it was, it was no casual traveller, he told himself.

Long, full minutes crept by as he waited, his eyes and ears straining against the heavy cloak of night. Aching with tension, he wondered if it had been something else he'd heard, his imagination playing tricks.

But then he heard the puffy snort of the horse, the light clip of its hoofs. So, who the hell are you, mister? he asked himself. As he was realizing what had happened, what was so different about the sound of the horse, he flinched from the bullet that smashed in to a branch just above his head. The sound of the gun cracked the night apart, resounded wildly along the road and up through the timberline.

Jack dropped from the saddle, made a grab for his Colt as he went down on to one knee. He was looking to his left and above him. He cursed, waited for another shot before the echo had died.

The sounds had been lighter from the horse because there'd been no rider. That man had already dismounted, had worked a rising loop through the brush. He'd be higher than Jack now, hugging the duff, trying to figure if he'd brought down his prey.

Jack felt a cramp, moved and felt the painful drag of a calf muscle. The chill had started, and his hands were sweating. With his left hand, he stretched his fingers into the soil, dug around until he touched a hard-packed fir cone. He grunted quietly and eased himself back to standing. Then he flexed his arm, sent the cone spinning into the brush, way off to his right.

The moment it crashed to ground, the man on the bank above Jack, fired; he couldn't afford not to. But Jack had set the trap, was the one waiting to pinpoint the flash of the gun.

The gelding was schooled well enough to stay ground-hitched. It would stomp testily, but not move off. Jack started firing as he lunged up the slope, as he made straight for the man who was in deadly pursuit of him.

The man heard him, and his next bullet thumped hard by Jack's neck. But Jack's blood was surging and he went on. With his hand out front of him, as if to ward off the bullets, he went crunching through the bed of needles and blowdown. Punching thunder, the guns were now almost on each other, their muzzle flashes searing the pitch blackness. He tilted full into a tree, swore and staggered sideways, firing again.

'I ain't always been a log splitter,' he seethed.

Then a gurgling cry tore from the shadows ahead, and the opposing gun stopped its deadly fusillade.

Jack dropped to a crouch. His heart was thumping, and his breath came in painful draughts. Ahead of him he heard a low groan, a final crash of woody bracken and then came the stillness.

I'm not for getting lured on by that, he thought, and waited out another ten, fifteen seconds. Then he moved forward, his Colt straight-armed ahead of him. He stopped when he knew he'd met up with his foe, when the toe of his boot contacted the sprawled, lifeless form.

He knew the man was dead when he dealt out a more probing kick. The touch cut him with a wave of sickness and he jerked his foot away, took a step back. He swallowed hard and pushed the Colt back into his holster. Then he pushed his hand inside his jacket to reach his cigarette makings and realized he was bleeding.

The wetness was oozing down his ribs, underneath his left arm. It wasn't a tree he'd run into, it was the bullet that had hit him. He felt little pain, just hollowness in the pit of his stomach. Cursing, he pushed his fingers to the patch of warm blood, where the lead has sliced him below the armpit. He flinched at the pain, but realized it was little more than a flesh wound. He struck a match across his gunbelt as he stepped forward again, crouched and held its flicker of light near to the dead man's face.

It was Hote Stuckley's partner, the man named Gruse. He was flat on his back, his eyes staring straight up, his skin pinched tight around his disagreeable features. His broad, waxen forehead was dashed with blood where Jack's bullet had taken away the top of his head.

Staring down, Jack muttered something fitting. 'I went to school with an ugly kid,' he recalled thoughtfully. 'He weren't o' your rank though. Someone attendin' shoulda drowned you at birth.'

Jack blew at the small flame, and stood, looked up at the stars. 'At least grizzlies an' mad dogs'll leave you be,' he said. 'But what of Mr Stuckley?' he added.

He shivered suddenly, curiously relieved it was Gruse, not Hote Stuckley he had killed. Nevertheless, his one-time friend could be out there in the night, ready to make his play at Jack. But Jack surmised that, if he was, he would already have drawn fire from him.

With some relief, he went back to the big spruce, and his gelding. As he emerged from the blackness, the horse snorted nervously, tossed its head and backed off.

'Hey, take it easy,' Jack offered, as soothingly as he could. 'Who were you expectin'?'

'The law,' a voice, reported from behind him. 'So don't do anythin' too hasty, Jack. We got any fancy move o' yours well covered.'

Jack braced himself, groaned inwardly then turned to face the sheriff. Elmer Redland's solid figure stepped from the deep shadows of the trees, but Jack knew he was just about surrounded.

'Bring the lantern up,' someone grunted.

Moments later, a big bull's eye threw light across the incident. Jack saw a half-dozen of the posse, their faces severe, blanched by the lantern glow. Carrying an array of guns, they were men he knew, and Ralph Rawlins stood grimly among them.

9

TAKEN IN

'Two o' you, go see if you can find the other scissor-bill,' Elmer Redland called out. 'Likely, he won't be makin' much noise.'

As the pair moved off, up through the trees, Redland moved stiffly towards Jack.

'Trailin's a poor business in these hills at best o' times,' he said. 'We'da turned back in another few minutes if you hadn't started up your own goddamn hostilities. Now is that bad luck for you, or what?'

'Well, bad luck's always been good for someone,' Jack started. 'Don't you go jumpin'–' But he was interrupted when one of the men spotted the leather pouches slung behind the gelding's saddle.

'Take a look there, Sheriff,' he called out. 'Them sure ain't flour bags.'

At that, Ralph Rawlins shouldered his way forward. He grabbed at the pouches, fumbled at the flaps with eager hands. 'By all ... it's here,' he cried hoarsely. 'This is the

Leesburg money.'

'It's no more'n a goddamn start, if it is. But a good 'un, I'll give you.' The sheriff pinned a chilly gaze on Jack. 'You gone an' got yourself arrested, Jack. An' that's enough to relieve you o' this,' he said, as he reached out, lifted the warm gun from his new prisoner's holster. 'You can explain some, on the way back to town.'

'I can explain now,' Jack said, feeling the pall of distrust. 'It's what I came after. I trailed 'em, just like you done me. Only difference is, I had to kill a man who didn't want to give it back ... the Leesburg payrolls. I reckoned on havin' another go at gettin' through.'

'O' course you were,' Redland said. 'An' I'm the man in the moon.'

Then Ralph Rawlins made his move. He pushed violently at Jack's chest, almost knocking him over. 'You rat,' he snorted wildly, '"It's my job to get the payrolls through", you said. Hah. To get through to the Harrow Bank, more like.'

'Steady,' Jack said sharply. 'Throwin' weight around ain't what you're good at.'

His mouth chewing with anger, Rawlins lashed out with his fist. There wasn't much steam behind the wild swing but it caught

Jack square in the face. The bony sting came in an instant, and Jack went for the return. But two of Redland's men grabbed at him, held his arms. He wrenched away half-heartedly, but it was for no gain. They hauled him back, let him breathe deep, stare an ominous hex on Rawlins.

'You really shouldn'ta' done that, Ralphy,' Jack said. 'Whatever you think, you've just lost your company a loyal hand.'

'Enough,' Redland decided impatiently. He looked out beyond the spread of the lamplight. 'Looks like someone got brought down from the top o' the hill.'

'He's a dead 'un,' one of the two returning men announced. Between them, they were dragging the body of Gruse. 'We messed him up some. But he could've looked like one we got a description of. A lean cove o' mean disposition, old Harve said.'

'There was two of 'em held up the stage,' somebody else said.

Redland looked back at his prisoner. 'Got anythin' to say?' he asked.

Jack gave him a vinegary look. 'Like what? I was there, remember?'

'That's just fine with me, boy.' The sheriff turned to his men. 'I'd say we got most o' what we came for. Get the horses, an' we'll

62

head off back.' He looked down at the grubby, roughed-up form of the dead man. 'He must've left a mount somewhere around here ... the best part of his worldly goods, I'll wager. See if you can find it, an' load him up. We'll go on, get Mr Harrow settled down safely for the night.'

And so Jack Harrow returned. It was first light when they clipped along the main street, pinky-grey feathers streaking the sky above Laurin Flats. The town boasted dual cells, beneath a small squared courthouse. Elmer Redland wasted no time in getting Jack booked in, secure behind a heavy wooden door that bore the branded legend, 'tomorrow never comes.'

Jack had said all he had to at that time, didn't bother with much else. Being caught in possession of saddle-bags that were jam-packed with stolen cash meant a great deal in the eyes of the law. When the sheriff had gone, Jack peered through the strap-iron bars into the adjoining cell.

A cowboy who was sleeping off bottle-fever, hawked and moved beneath a lousy blanket. Jack shuddered, it was the first time he'd seen the inside of a jail. He squinted at the scarred walls, then slowly stretched out on the narrow cot. He clasped his hands, held them under his head. There was a single, high set window that looked out at street level to the lifting day beyond. He was bushed from hours in the saddle, queasy from the emptiness in his belly. But the tiredness was conditioned, and it stopped him from sleep. He could only lie there and brood upon his plight, the times past, the grim future. At best he'd get a trial lawyer. Laurin Flats drew on the services of a father and son practice. Yep, that would be about it, he thought wearily. The old one wouldn't care and the youngster wouldn't know. But either one of them would be up to delving into the past, find out what Jack had been up to, prior to him taking over his family's fencing business. The very best legal representatives couldn't build much of a defence when that little lot rose against him. Jack closed his eyes against the bleakness. He knew that those few who would have spoken up for him before, would walk away now.

10

MIXED SIGNS

Crawford Menroe shifted his bones in the saddle. Ditched a weary look at Nell Yuman. 'Well, this is just about where it happened. Now you goin' to tell me what's goin' on?'

The girl looked doubtfully at the rugged timberline that climbed about them, the pass through which they'd followed the winding route of the Rawlins coach. 'That's what we're here for ... to find out,' she said. 'Oh hell, I don't know.' She opened and closed her fist on the horn of her saddle. 'But if you're certain this is the place...'

The old cowpuncher hunched his shoulders. 'See them marks?' His rope-scarred hand pointed to the dust at their horses' feet. 'It was a lot o' riders stirred that up. An' yonder...' He swung his arm toward the scrubby slope above the road. 'That's where the shootin' must've been ... where they took him.' Menroe looked tiredly at Nell. 'What we goin' to make out o' this place, missy? Maybe we should start back,' he grumbled. 'I'm too old to go bustin' these hills. I'll be stove up, with your pa shoutin' ... probably firin' me, for helpin' you go chasin' that owlhoot, Harrow.'

'He'll only know, if I tell him, Craw. An' I certainly will, if you don't help me. You can read sign as good as any scout. So get them marks *unstirred* ... tell me what you see.'

Menroe dragged off his hat, ran the flat of his hand across his iron-grey stubbly hair. His skin was a dark copper colour, and sun lines etched deep into the corners of his eyes and mouth. He pushed his hat back, and blinked fiercely a few times. Nell watched him push stiff knuckles into his forehead as he deliberated.

After a moment, Menroe sniffed loudly and nodded, mumbled an OK. Then, he twisted down from the saddle, nudged his mare and started off down the coach road. He looked carefully at the marks he found in the dust as they walked away from the pass.

Nell wanted to follow but not wanting to cross Menroe's path or mess the sign any more, she stayed where she was.

It seemed an age before Menroe came back. He didn't look up, just walked on past.

Then he pulled the mare to one side, put her up the shallow bank and halted beneath a big, blue spruce. He dismounted and squatted down, made a careful note of the findings. He lifted his head, and took a long speculative glance at the slope above him, before straightening with a grimace.

'This is where Harrow left his mount,' he said, returning to where Nell was still waiting patiently. 'He woulda chose the big Engelmann for cover. He was headed this way–'

'This way?' she broke in. 'Back to Laurin Flats? How sure can you be, Craw?'

'Certain sure. Also,' he went on, 'two hundred yards downslope there's some overlyin' prints. There was another horse followin' Harrow's, an' at a rate.'

'What's it all mean, Craw?' Nell asked.

'I'd say this other feller knew he'd been spotted. Harrow probably heard him,' Menroe continued with a small, crafty smile. 'He left his mount, took off into the brush, circled above where Harrow would've been.'

'What happened?'

'Well, he got himself killed. Harrow nailed him.'

Nell leaned from the saddle, gripped a bony shoulder through Menroe's faded shirt. 'You ain't just guessin', are you, Craw?

I know you weren't up here to see it.'

Menroe made a trivializing gesture. 'Hell, the *sign's* here to see, Miss Nell,' he said. 'If it had been any newer, I coulda told you when he last took a bath.'

'Well, whatever's there gets to clear Jack's name,' Nell suggested.

'An' how'd you figure that?'

'Why else would he have been on this road, unless he was returnin' the payrolls? That makes sense, don't it?' she asked when Menroe didn't answer.

The trace of a scowl cut across Menroe's weathered face. 'Now who's guessin'?' he said, and shambled back to his mare, tugged at the belly strap.

Nell narrowed her eyes, looked thoughtfully at Menroe as he pulled himself back into his saddle.

'"Let a dog have its day", you said, Craw. Are you still holdin' somethin' against him?' she said disappointedly.

'Reckon you're the one holdin' somethin', missie, an' I was talkin' about *dogs*. Jack Harrow's always been a bad 'un, an' there's a pile of evidence still pointin' that way. That's all I got to say.'

'Fine,' Nell retorted. 'Now, let's get back home.'

11

ON THE LOOSE

Beneath the courthouse. Jack Harrow was having a talk with Barclay Kittle. Jack was pacing back and forth across the unpleasantly chill cell, while the attorney perched on the edge of the cot. When Jack had given his account of events, his part in it, the old man leaned forward, spat brown juice onto the hard-packed floor.

'I'm thinkin' of advisin' you to escape,' he pronounced flatly. 'If it was me tryin' your case, I'd be considerin' hard labour.'

'You won't be representin' me then?' Jack suggested wryly.

'Best send for Kittle the younger. Not that he'll get you very far.'

'Then I'll do my own talkin',' Jack said coldly.

The men stopped talking as footsteps sounded outside the cell. Elmer Redland threw a bolt, pulled open the heavy door.

'Come out here,' he said. 'I want to talk to

69

you ... got some things to discuss.'

'Who you talkin' to?' Jack asked.

'*You*. I'm talkin' to *you*.'

'You already asked me if I had anythin' to say ... you an' the hangin' judge here. Me bein' innocent don't seem to figure in either o' your wits.'

Redland shared an uneasy look with Kittle. 'Yeah, well, maybe I done some thinkin'. Like, why it was you ran out on me yesterday afternoon.'

'Hah, 'cause I had good reason,' Jack retorted. 'Harvey Maud had got himself a story. He'd notioned some hokum piece of evidence about me an' the hold up. He was goin' to kick me in the pit, or get *you* to do it. But I was answerable, an' wanted a crack at returnin' the money.'

Redland considered Jack's answer. 'Them's fine sentiments from a shotgun rider,' he said. 'But sentiment's one thing, an' actions is another. You went up, deep into the trees an' got the drop on them two buckos, while givin' me an' my men the run around?'

'Yeah, you know I did. Put it down to my good luck an' your bad trackin'.'

'Then, single-handed you braced 'em, an' grabbed the money?' Redland made a further incredulous enquiry. 'Weren't there some time when you thought to try an' hold 'em, let them do the explainin'?'

Jack shook his head. 'Nope. I don't draw pay for that sort o' work, Sheriff. That's your territory. My job's guardin' ... gettin' the boxes through. I ain't saddled with any concern after that ... just ask Rawlins.'

The sheriff cupped his chin in his hand. 'Your story's got more goddamn holes than a hazer's pants,' he muttered wistfully. 'There's a whole heap o' stuff you ain't touchin' on.'

'What goddamn "heap o' stuff"?' Jack was snapping out his frustration, wobbling between fact and fiction. 'I was bringin' the payrolls back. In so doin' I had to kill one of 'em who tried to stop me,' he continued. 'That's the meat of it, Sheriff. Now, are you lettin' me go or what?'

Redland's eyebrows raised. He nodded slowly. 'Yeah,' he admitted, 'reckon I might have to. After all, I got nothin' but Maud's story, an' he was only supposin' ... imaginin'. But there's just one more thing ... lawman's curiosity I guess. Exactly what was it gave you wind o' that feller fixin' to bushwhack you?'

Jack frowned. 'I heard a noise. You know, the sound of a bullet chewin' out the branch

71

of an Engelmann pine. When it nearly takes your ear off, it kind o' gives the game away.'

The sheriff puffed his own exasperation, and swung the cell door wide. 'Rawlins says he ain't pressin' a charge. An' as you ain't indicted for anythin' else, there's no deal I can hold you on. You're a free man again.'

The situation was getting beyond Jack who was past caring, and he wasn't about to stay and contend anything. He angled a look at Barclay Kittle, 'Thanks, Lawyer, nice to have made your acquaintance,' he said, and twisted his mouth with a derisive smile. 'You're a credit to the legal profession.'

The sheriff gave his own advice as Jack stepped past him. 'Stay out o' trouble,' he offered. 'You ain't gettin' no legal help hereabouts.'

'I never was, Sheriff,' Jack returned.

The cowboy in the adjoining cell crawled from his blanket, went from hands and knees to standing and followed them out into the short corridor. He looked around, shook his roostered head uncomprehendingly.

'You know what day this is?' Jack asked him with a grin.

'Can't recall the goddamn year,' the man rasped, then continued an unsteady walk up the steps towards the early sunshine.

At street level, in the small jail office, Redland nodded to a deputy. The man took Jack's belt and Colt from a drawer and handed them over. He looked closely at the other gun Jack had been carrying. 'Yours, too?' he asked. 'This curious piece of ordnance?'

Jack nodded. 'Strictly speakin' it belongs to the haulage company. I'll return it to 'em,' he said, and took the gun, pushed it back into his coat pocket. Then he strapped his gunbelt in place, dragged on his hat and took to the outside.

On the rough, puncheoned walkway, three men stood silhouetted against the rising sun. They turned abruptly when Jack appeared.

One of them was the sheriff, the other two were Ralph Rawlins and Crawford Menroe. Jack gave Menroe a questioning glance, wondered what the old 'puncher was doing and got a stony look in return.

Rawlins cleared his throat, hesitated in finding his voice. 'Ah, Jack,' he started, awkwardly.

But Jack wasn't considerate of Ralph Rawlins' unease. He stood silent, unmoving, except for the scar tissue beneath his eye. Then, under a few days' stubble, his jaw decided to remind him of Rawlins' fist.

'Jack,' Rawlins blundered on, 'I guess you'd say there's been a misunderstandin' ... a *big* misunderstandin'. I know you were bringin' the cash in. My head got the better of me, got to sayin' other things for a while. But now we got everythin' back, let's start over, what d'you say?'

Jack was thinking about Rawlins' last words to him. He recalled the distrust, the nasty zeal of the man's eyes.

'What do you say, Jack?' Rawlins persisted. 'Are you comin' back to work for me ... the Rawlins set-up? Can you put all this behind you?'

'Well, are you?' Redland asked, after a moment or two, getting the nature of Jack's silence.

Jack took himself a long, slow breath, looked at Redland. 'Reckon I ain't a "turn the other cheek" sort o' feller, Sheriff,' he said. 'An' if it's any concern o' yours, my answer's no, on both counts.'

Jack then turned his attention back to Rawlins. 'Your way's too easy, Rawlins ... too convenient. You accuse an' threat, an' if you get backed into a corner, just say it's some sort o' misunderstandin' an' every-thin's to be forgot. Well, I'll tell you what the misunderstandin' is, mister, it's you *thinkin'* it gets forgot.'

Rawlins' sweating face lost more colour, as Jack took a step towards him. He shook when he realized that this time Elmer Redland wasn't going to intervene.

But Jack didn't strike out. 'I ain't goin' to forget you puttin' your knuckles to my face, nor your off-beam accusations,' he said. 'If you ever cross me again, you'll end up as a piece o' trail kill.'

12

MEETING TIME

Some time after dusk, Jack came down from his room. He'd rested, felt better for washing away the cling of cell damp. When he crossed the lobby into the McRae's dining-room, he sensed the stir. He surveyed the spread of tables from the swagged doorway, noticed that no one in the room would meet his eye directly.

Parker Meeling pushed back his chair, was rising to leave just as Jack entered. The Rawlins clerk hesitated momentarily, another who was reluctant to meet face to face. But Jack had something to say, gave him no choice from where he stood.

'Seen anythin' o' Rawlins ... your boss?' Jack asked, as Meeling approached.

'No.' The reply carried the clerk's usual surliness, but now there was a dash of fear in his eyes.

'I want to see him. Tell him to meet me in the bar, at nine,' Jack said.

'I'm no messenger of yours, Harrow,' Meeling retorted.

'You're who the hell I say you are, Meelin'. Go tell him,' he barked.

The clerk glared his distaste. But when Jack moved, he edged through the doorway to the lobby, then straight out the front door.

Jack knew the exchange with Meeling was shared, and this time he met prying stares from the dining-room. Within an hour, most of the town would be making what they would from his demand of Ralph Rawlins. He sat in one corner of the room, relaxed and tried to enjoy his meal. Precious McRae held no truck with customers prejudiced against Jack, even storeyed up the fried chicken pieces. As he sipped his coffee, his thoughts turned to Rachel Rawlins. He wondered if it was a failing, if it was something he'd regret.

It was night dark proper, when Jack left the boarding-house. The town seemed oddly quiet and not a breath of wind stirred. The crisp air felt clean, but he sensed he still carried the sour whiff of the cell. He looked up and down the street. 'Goddamn stink must be in my whiskers,' he muttered to himself, and walked to the haircutter's, where a light still shone.

'Too late,' the barber said, as soon as Jack's entrance pinged the bell above his door.

Jack looked beyond the cutter's big chair. 'So, hang another lamp,' he replied. 'I'll rack me a game.'

The haircutter had a pool table out back, and under the spreading lamplight, Jack rolled a yellowing ball across the baize. He pulled a cue from its frame, and sighted the crushed tip towards the pack.

'You want some chalk for that?' the cutter asked, his voice doubtful, as if Jack's answer would determine how long he was staying.

'Get yourself closed up,' Jack told him. 'I'll leave peaceable when you're ready.'

For a few minutes, Jack snapped balls into the pockets, enjoyed the startlingly loud noise in the hanging silence. He looked up when he heard the doorbell ping again, grounded the butt end of his cue when he saw Ormer Pugg.

Under the light from the front part of the shop, Jack noticed that the man's mouth was still puffed-up and discoloured from the punch he'd dealt him two nights ago. The haircutter stared worriedly from one man to the other.

Jack nodded. 'You lookin' to play pool?' he asked, letting his right hand drop to the butt of his Colt.

Pugg held out his arms, shook his head. 'Nope. I saw you come in, wondered if you'd thought any more about that pro-position o' mine?'

Slowly, Jack looked up. 'No,' he said, 'can't say I have. But then up until a few hours ago, I had all the work I can handle. Besides, I told you I weren't interested.'

'Yeah, I remember. But I meant what I said ... still do.'

'What is it you really want me to do for you, Pugg?' Jack demanded. 'You're wantin' me to take that Gruse feller's place? Is that it?'

Pugg's broad face pulled an uncompre-hending look. 'I don't want you to be fillin' anyone's place. Who the hell's Gruse?'

'The hold-up man who just got his saddle sent home.'

Pugg shook his head. 'I know nothin' o' that. But I do know you're off the Rawlins' payroll. That's why I'm talkin' to you again.'

'Right this minute, payroll talk don't interest me. An' I can't think what your need for me is, unless it's to ride shotgun on Hote Stuckley ... keep him away from the wrong stages. He weren't too pleased with me walkin' off with his saddle-bags.'

'I don't understand why you're tyin' me in with this robbery,' Pugg said. 'An' I never heard o' Stuckley or Gruse.'

Jack knew he was lying, but the man held a stoic expression.

'I'm competin' with Rawlins Haulage,' Pugg persisted. 'I got a crew to start erectin' barns, an' fencin' up a wagon yard. There's two coaches an' a line o' freighters already on the way here, an' I've sent a man out to Bozeman for horses an' mules. I told you, Harrow, I'm startin' this proper, an' it ain't too late to come in.'

Jack smiled tiredly. 'It don't make sense to go into business where there ain't any. An' we ain't goin' to reach agreement on your way o' creatin' it. So, while I'm tryin' to think of another way to say "no", why don't you put that fencin' contract my way? That's my other line o' work, in case you forgot.'

Ormer Pugg's persistence finally cracked. 'You're a disappointment, Harrow,' he said. 'I guess you really ain't the *hombre* I had in mind, an' from what I hear, it's just about comin' up to provin' time.'

As Pugg turned his back and walked off, Jack looked at the banjo clock that was hanging at the rear of the narrow building. It looked like two minutes off nine o'clock.

80

The haircutter was watching him intently. 'That clock's ten minutes fast, son, you don't need to hurry,' he said. 'Then again, you don't want to be late, do you?' he added with a devious twist.

Jack lifted his cue, rolled it hard across the table and cursed. He'd been right. All the town knew of his enticement to Rawlins.

13

NO SHOW

Other than an occasional wedge of light from a door or window, the main street of Laurin Flats was as dark and deserted as it had been earlier in the evening.

The deadness of the town wasn't unusual for the middle of the week, so Jack was surprised when he pushed through the side door of the bar that was annexed to McRae's boarding-house.

It was a brightly lit and near to full. Some of the customers were townspeople, others 'punchers from nearby spreads. Hard to say where they'd all come from, but they weren't all there for the drinking. Those that were actually holding their glasses, held them still when Jack entered. Then they glanced sheepishly around them, embarrassed to be suddenly confronted with the reason for them being there.

But nobody ventured to leave and, as the door juddered shut, a stunned hush fell across the muggy room.

Jack gave no more than a glance at any of the faces about him as he moved to the L-shaped bar. At the short end, a space cleared, and he settled a forearm onto the glossy, dark wood, nodded to the ready barkeep for a glass and bottle. He slowly filled the glass to its rim, pushed the bottle to one side and steadily lifted the drink. He saw his reflection in the back bar, the nervous expressions on the faces that were watching him fixedly. Well, this'll show 'em, he thought ... no nerves.

Above the string of beer jugs and whiskey bottles, there was a clock the minute hand of which clunked upright at nine o'clock precisely. It was as though time had frozen itself as Jack had walked from the pool hall. The haircutter's banjo timepiece had showed him exactly the same thing.

Jack swallowed his whiskey, clicked the empty glass alongside the bottle. Turning then, he saw the men in the room look to the door that led out front. He squared himself, nodded acknowledgement as Elmer Redland walked towards him.

Redland pushed up tight to Jack, his features set sternly. 'Don't tell me you're here for a quiet drink,' he said without preamble.

'Whatever you got on your mind, just forget it. I could arrest you right now.'

'For what?' Jack immediately wanted to know.

The sheriff eyed Jack warily. 'How about, behavin' in a manner likely to breach the peace?'

'I got myself a room full of eyewitnesses, Sheriff. Ain't one of 'em seen me do more'n lift a glass. Ask 'em.'

'You know what I'm talkin' about,' Redland insisted. 'Goddamn town an' country knows why you're here.'

Jack had a quick glance around him, half smiled and shook his head. 'Yeah, well not everyone's *turned up*, eh, Sheriff.'

'Perhaps we'd all rest easy if I put you back in that cell,' Redland suggested half-heartedly. 'What in hell's name were you goin' to do? Shoot him?'

Jack brought up his small, tired smile again. 'I don't know, I never did. What do you do with a louse, squash 'em, put a match to their ass? Maybe I was goin' to ridicule him in front o' this crowd, his customers? I spent a long night in that hole 'cause o' Ralph Rawlins.'

The sheriff realized that Jack wasn't in killing humour. 'Yeah, I know you did,' he said, a little more considerately. 'But you got to remember the man was out of his head with worry, didn't know what he was doin' or sayin'. He stood to lose everythin'.'

'An' stupidity don't know no limits,' Jack sneered. 'He could be somewhere out there right now, lyin' up for me. I wouldn't put a backshot past him. So we all get to stay for another drink. You too, Sheriff?'

Redland looked up at the clock above the bar, then levelled a scowl at each of the exits; to the walkway out front, to the side street, the private staff door to the boarding-house's lobby. 'He sure ain't comin' here,' he said, by way of an answer, and Jack thought he saw the shadow of disappointment cross his face. 'An' this ain't no goddamn frontier gun town. But I still got places to watch over,' was Redland's obvious warning.

Jack shrugged. 'Almost too much for one man,' he said enigmatically, digging into his pants pocket. He slapped coin onto the bar to pay for his drink and started for the front doorway. Behind him, the sheriff snapped, 'Where you goin' now?'

'Wherever lice go to die,' Jack retorted. He paced through the milling customers, made for the walkway before the sheriff had time to respond.

Jack stood outside of the bar for a moment. He brushed away a buckeye moth, spat some of the distaste from his mouth and took a deep breath of fresh air. 'Damn the lot o' you,' he muttered.

Jack took another lungful of crisp cold air, felt the tension lift from his chest and shoulders. He had no intention or wish to find Rawlins now. His attitude towards the man had settled into cold disdain, a matter suddenly over and done with.

He heard someone move through the shale path, out of the cottonwoods. He turned, watched a man edge towards him from the deep shadow of McRae's. It was one of the town drunks, a derelict who'd run errands for the price of a shot of rotgut whiskey.

'Word's out you're lookin' for Rawlins,' the man said. 'Well, he ain't in town, 'cause I seen him … seen him leave.' The sot waited, showed his teeth in a dry-mouthed leer.

Jack took the news almost without hearing it. 'Wonder who he was tryin' to avoid, you or me?' he said, abstractedly.

'I thought you'd want to know, Mr Harrow.' The voice of the man from the shadows became a gripe. 'I didn't have no need to tell you. *Et tu Brute*,' he added, as a booze-clouded tilt from some long ago teaching,

Jack turned to take a closer look at the man, caught the whiff of soiled clothes and rancid breath. With a snort of disgust, he hauled up a dollar, and flicked it. The man made a scramble for it in the shale, mumbled a sort of gratitude, something about watching out.

'Interestin' way to make a day's wages,' Jack gave out. 'Grovellin', an' not quite knowin' for what.' Then he turned away, started to make for the boarding-house's staircase.

'Yeah, damn 'em all,' he rumbled on again. He thought he'd have another crack at his business, build it up as his pa would have, or should have. Perhaps he'd erect a mill with a roof, get a team to operate scroll saws, start to fence-in eastern Montana. 'I could make my own goddamn coffin,' he said to himself.

It was late, but Jack was eager to get his traps, and check out of town. For some time he'd been working with no real point or purpose. He'd learned that dissatisfaction down one road didn't meant satisfaction was inevitably waiting down another. But now he'd had his mind made up for him, he took the staircase up to his room two at a time.

Owing to the Mrs McRae quirk about no locks on doors, it led to boarders thinking twice about leaving valuables in their rooms; although Jack thought that anyone with a mind to stealing from him, was welcome to whatever they found. He twisted the handle and pushed the door open, stood staring in uncertainty and puzzlement across the glow of the table lamp. Rachel Rawlins was sitting on the edge of the mattress.

Dressed in working duds, the girl rose quickly. She had her hair tucked into the crown of a plainsman's hat, would go almost unnoticed in the dark. 'Hello, Jack,' she said, in a trembly voice.

Jack stepped into the room, with uncertainty closed the door. He stood looking, thinking, the fascination of her eating into him. 'Your brother send you, did he? Lend you his vest an' pants for the occasion?' he added, as a needless sting.

Rachel shook her head slowly as she looked Jack in the eye. 'And you're the one to judge him, are you?' she asked.

Jack shrugged, looked around his room as if to discover someone else there. 'He's a spineless ingrate. That ain't judgin' him,' he answered her.

Rachel looked down at her tightly clasped

hands for a moment, before responding. 'There's a lot o' folk held with what he done an' said, Jack. Most of 'em would call it normal. He ain't out o' the same pod as you, that's all. Remember, Ralph ain't the one who's askin' you to let him be. *I am.*'

'Look around you, Rachel. This is about workin' for Rawlins Haulage,' Jack said harshly. 'For a while, I really thought I'd be gettin' me a bit more satisfaction, an opportunity with Rawlins Haulage, but I was wrong. I reckon home's the resort o' them things. I just couldn't see it. So, if shieldin' your brother's why you come here, it weren't necessary. My mind's made up, an' he don't figure.'

Rachel rose from the mattress, took a step towards Jack. 'I came here to ask you to come back an' work for us,' she said. 'Ralph failed at that, too, didn't he?'

'Yeah, you're goddamn right he did. 'Cause the answer's *no*, Rachel. Forget it.'

Rachel came straight to him, placed a hand on his arm. 'Please reconsider, Jack,' she appealed. 'I wouldn't ask if there was any other way. It was because o' you we got the payrolls back. But next time ... if you're not...'

'Why should there be a next time?' Jack speculated.

'Because there's someone out there. Some-one called Ormer Pugg. You know it, the whole town knows it. He's out to cripple Rawlins Haulage. We need more than a shot-gun guard, we need *you*. If Owen Treebucks loses even one shipment, we're finished. Can't you at least think about it?'

Jack wasn't ready to succumb to Rachel Rawlins. 'Go to Garrison, an' hire yourself an ex-trooper.'

'I could, but that's too mercenary. We ... *I* need more than that.' Rachel sniffed and shook her head. Jack saw the glint of a tear, sensed the persuasive screw start its turn.

'I've got to have someone I can depend on. He's got to be reliable, an' loyal, an' good enough to fight. They're virtues that you hold, Jack. Neither me or Ralph are coach shootists.'

Jack laughed, heard Ormer Pugg's words echoing around his head. 'Showed a weak-ness', the man had forewarned.

'Yeah, all right,' he ceded. 'I'll ride your coaches until I decide not to. That'll more'n likely be when your brother gets to buggin' me again. Go tell him.'

Even as he spoke, Jack heard more echoes; his own, recalling his decision to ride away, and the drunk who wanted to sell him the whereabouts of Ralph Rawlins. Nothing was right about any of it he knew, as Rachel's arm moved up to his neck. The feeling of unease was too great and he eased away.

'Go tell him *now*, wherever he's burrowed, before I change my mind.' Jack saw Rachel's jaw trembling with emotion, but he couldn't think for who or what. He opened the door and stood aside. 'Goodnight, Rachel, an' watch the steps,' he said, still retaining his true feelings.

'Wouldn't want the townsfolk knowin', if I took a tumble,' she quipped back.

Five minutes later, Jack was stuffing his meagre belongings into his war bag. For the time being, he'd had enough of Laurin Flats. Now the infinite darkness and solitude of the open land seemed good.

14

FEW WARNINGS

From first light, Jack laboured at the sawing and paring of juniper. Toward noon, a brawny wind pushed grey cloud across the sky, and for two hours it rained. For a man shaping rails and props, it was miserable work, with the water running down the neck of his slicker, inside his sleeves. But mid-afternoon, the cloud broke, the rain stopped and the earth steamed under a late, slanting sun.

Come nightfall, Jack felt as though he'd accomplished the work of two men. 'Nothin' much changin' hereabouts,' he muttered wryly, as he built a cigarette before cleaning up.

His stoical mood suffered a setback when, riding into the lamplit town, he noticed the building set back from the livery. It was a broad, open-fronted shed, that had only ever been used as a site for travelling quacks and salesmen to post their broadsides. But this night, the interior was strung with happy jack lanterns, and through the wide front opening, Jack could see two Concord coaches standing alongside each other. They weren't the latest models – a painter was sitting on a barrel, renovating the painted scenes on the door panels – and Jack knew they weren't for Rawlins Haulage.

He rode on to the livery, where the town's half-bake who served as a nightman greeted him with an excited stamp of his foot.

'You saw 'em did you, Mr Harrow ... saw them ol' Pitchin' Betsies?' he asked. 'They'll be racin' the Rawlins' stock, eh? You ridin' for 'em or what, Mr Harrow?'

Jack didn't want to get drawn into a wit-sapping conversation. 'I'm totin' a gun for Rawlins Haulage, Harve,' he said. 'Same as I've always done.'

Harve puffed a bit. 'Folks say this Pugg's sittin' on a pot o' gold, Mr Harrow. Sup-posin' he wants to battle you?'

Jack smiled. 'You certainly get to see an' hear plenty, don't you, Harve? If only it weren't so late, I'd stop an' find out how much.'

Harve laughed loudly. 'Miss Rachel said it didn't matter much; she weren't goin' to lose nothin'.'

'You been talkin' to Miss Rachel?' Jack asked a little sharply.

But the boy indicated that Jack avail himself of the livery service. He laughed again and started to shamble away, his head buzzing with things only half understood.

Jack stared after him. He swore, wondered where he was off to, what Rachel could have meant.

Ten minutes later, Jack made for Humble's. The mercantile store was open to cater for a small number of late customers. He crossed the main street, walked up the steps that fronted the lamp-bright building. He'd almost reached the door when a girl came out, a man either side of her, Jack stopped because it was Nell Yuman, and he acknowledged her, touched the brim of his hat.

She hesitated for a moment, then, without responding, she turned aside and hurried on past him along the walkway. Jack was about to call after her with a fitting appeal when, from the doorway, a voice rasped his name.

He turned around, as Nell's father, Jerome Yuman, and Crawford Menroe stepped forward. Where the lantern beside the door threw light on their faces, Jack could see that their usual august looks now held a taut anger.

'Stay away from Nell. She ain't speakin' with you,' Yuman spoke again.

'Yeah, so it would seem. I would have appreciated hearing it from *her* though,' Jack retorted. He frowned, looked from one to another of the men who stood before him. 'You makin' her utterances now are you, Mr Yuman?' he added.

Before Yuman could answer, Menroe cut in. 'Are you goin' back to work for Rawlins, after your promise to kill him?' he challenged.

'I never promised anythin'. An' no one ever heard me do so,' Jack shot back.

The two men exchanged glances. 'But I guess the rest of it's true,' Yuman said.

'What "rest of it"?' Jack said.

'That Rachel Rawlins spent some time in your room last night. She was seen on the steps.'

Jack sucked the air between his teeth. It was what the drunk meant about watching out, he realized. 'I know an' old goat who's gettin' paid from both ends,' he answered Yuman. 'Right now, he's makin' more money than you *or* me.'

Yuman eyed him coldly. 'The word's all over town. Who put it out, don't matter. Even a goddamn cheese-brain can see the price o' you an' Rawlins Haulage teamin' up again.'

Jack wanted to smile. He didn't know *who* the remark said most about – himself, Rachel, or Yuman for saying it.

'Poor ol' Taylor Rawlins'd be breakin' out of his coffin, if he knew what was happenin' here,' Yuman continued.

'Yeah, well, the dead ain't concernin' us right now,' Menroe put in. 'We just got to see that your Nell ain't bothered by this here feller.' For a moment, Menroe hesitated, then he went on, 'Damn you, Harrow. I shoulda kept my nose out o' your affairs ... let 'em railroad you on the hold-up charge.'

Jack exchanged a sharp, icy look with Menroe. He remembered the man had been with Ralph Rawlins and the sheriff outside of the jailer's office yesterday morning on his release. 'You had somethin' to do with me bein' freed?' he asked.

'If I did, it was for Nell, not you.'

'I guess it's clear now where we all stand,' Yuman said quietly.

'Never any doubt,' Jack granted, his tone clipped and fractious. 'An' if you think so little o' Rachel Rawlins, tell her to her face next time. Just make sure I get to see you do it,' he glowered.

'The only thing you'll be gettin' to see, Harrow, is the road out o' Laurin Flats.'

With those words, Yuman swung away from Jack. Menroe trailed him, and neither of them looked back. Jack stood for a moment, stewing with emotions, wondering where Nell had gone. Then he heeled around, opened the door into the lamplit interior of the mercantile store.

The tang of new leather and turpentine greeted him immediately, then the sweeter aromas of molasses and loose tobaccos. Either side of the long counter, a couple of oldsters were exchanging casual banter, dribbling cracker crumbs on to bolts of cloth. As Jack closed the door, they swung their rheumy eyes in his direction, like the customers of McRae's bar, not so long ago.

Jack swore under his breath, considered putting a bullet into the ceiling for effect. He handed his goods order to Wes Humble's shift storeman who hovered sheepishly at the opposite end of the counter. The man was ill at ease, making a pained effort not to show it. He made no attempt at the small talk one would normally exchange with a regular customer.

Ah, what the hell, no law says you got to be friends, Jack thought. 'I'll collect that stuff in a couple o' days. Have it ready,' he demanded. Then he walked from the store, his thoughts and mood unreadable.

15

THE RIVAL LINE

Jack started walking, made for the edge of town, for the old house that was Taylor Rawlins' dubious legacy to his children. He wanted to see Rachel, didn't want any misunderstanding about who was posting scurrilous rumours around town.

He trod the weed-grown path that led up to the porch. At the front door he pulled the bell cord and waited, shuffled his feet. A shadow fell across the coloured glass that filled the door window, the latch turned and Ralph Rawlins stood in the threshold.

It was the first time they'd seen each other since outside of the jailer's office, the day before. Jack thought the man's sullen face took on some colour, but he made no move to ease the moment, just held the moment.

Rawlins faltered into a backwards step. 'Owen Treebucks's here, too,' he mumbled diffidently.

'Really?' Jack said, wondering if he'd

99

chosen the wrong time. He stepped into the house, and as he hung his Stetson on a hall stand, Rawlins pushed the door to, behind him.

The parlour was filled with big furniture, from a time when it cost old man Rawlins a stack of hard-earned dollars to ship from Baltimore or Boston.

'Hello, Jack.' Rachel rose from a wing-back chair, offered her favoured greeting with an almost demure smile.

With one hand gripping the broad mantel-piece, Owen Treebucks nodded his greeting. Jack thought someone should drop a spill to the grate, put some conviviality into the room.

'Perhaps Mr Harrow ... Jack would like to hear what you've got to say,' Rachel addressed the Leesburg Mine manager.

'Well, it's not that I wanted to, you understand, but after seein' Mr Pugg, I had to think over what he said.'

'Pugg? What's he got to do with anythin' that we're involved in?' Jack asked, with feigned surprise.

'He's tryin' to get the Leesburg account. He's goin' to outbid us, that's what,' Ralph answered from the doorway.

'Yeah, can't say I hadn't heard,' Jack said,

again not expressing the entire truth.

'I haven't made any decision yet,' Treebucks said. 'I don't want to be the one responsible for harmin' the Rawlins Haulage, 'cause I know it would. I've only ever got first-rate service from you good folk. Up until recently, that is,' he added uneasily.

There was something in Treebucks' demeanour, a falsity that Jack didn't like.

'What do you mean by that?' he cut in. 'You lost one shipment, an' got it back.'

'I know that,' Treebucks said. 'It's the ... er delay, that was worryin'.'

Jack was about to say that whatever Treebucks had heard, he must have known that it was stupid and unfounded speculation, but Rachel threw him a glance which meant, don't.

'So what kind of copper-bottomed proposition is it that Mr Pugg's offerin'?' she asked of Treebucks. 'He must have spun you some story.'

For his account of what happened, Treebucks looked repeatedly between Jack and Rachel and Ralph Rawlins. 'Pugg came to my office this afternoon, told me he planned to establish a stage and freight line into the Beaverheads,' he explained. 'A line to rival yours. None o' that's news though, it's been general knowledge hereabouts for days. We've all seen the coaches he's renovatin' ... the wagon yards he's puttin' up. I said it was a shaky investment, 'cause we already got a well-established company in Rawlins Haulage. But he had more to say.'

'What?' Jack interrupted, without looking to Rachel who was glaring at Treebucks. At the same time, Jack was suddenly wondering about Owen Treebucks; a man who, although not the sharpest or shrewdest of men, could still make deals with whoever he wished, moreover, a man without need to stand in a contractor's parlour justifying himself.

But Jack sensed they were on the front foot. 'What was it?' he pushed.

Treebucks dragged out a handkerchief and ran it around his neck, fingering under the tight collar. 'Pugg claims that what happened to one o' your coaches, can happen again. An' at the end o' the day,' he said, with a quick nod at Jack, 'you're only the one set o' guns. Pugg says, that ain't enough to guard my payroll shipments.'

'Huh,' Jack grunted in disbelief. 'Seems to me, there's a lot more'n Pugg's wishful thinkin' in that story. You finished it yet?'

'No, not quite,' Treebucks said. 'He guarantees there'll be no trouble if I go with his outfit. He'll hire outriders for every stretch o' the road between here an' Fishtrap. He'll put out twenty men if he has to.'

'Twenty? Twenty gunmen? An' who'd you suppose takes care o' their pay ... Santa Claus?' Rachel snapped.

'Probably cost a tad more'n the payroll,' Jack suggested drily. 'Makes real good business sense.'

Treebucks shook his head gloomily. 'I said, I ain't decided yet. But it *is* a guarantee.'

'O' course it's guaranteed,' Jack answered back. 'For God's sake man, he's out to bleed your company. You'll end up same as Rawlins here. Pugg'll have taken so much o' the Leesburg value, he'll be buyin' you both up at bottom dollar.'

'What do *you* suggest then, Jack?' Ralph asked, moving forward tentatively.

'Jack Harrow. He'll be givin' you his own blue-chip, fur-trimmed pledge to get the next shipment through ... every last grain of it.'

'An' for that...?' Ralph started.

'I'll take five per cent of each an' every delivery. An' that's my price for comin' back to work for you, Ralph.'

'Not quite so fast, Mr Harrow. If I decide to stay with Rawlins Haulage, why are you so sure of gettin' the money through?' Treebucks wanted to know.

'Same reason Pugg's usin' for why we *won't*,' Jack replied without any further explanation.

All eyes were on him now, anxious and doubting.

'You ain't givin' us more than that?' Ralph questioned.

'Well, there just might be another reason for me taken' on Ormer Pugg,' Jack conceded. 'But that's between me, him an' the gate-post. How soon do you want the payroll through?' he asked Treebucks.

'Tomorrow,' the man said. 'The men at the mine are still waitin' to get paid.'

'Yeah, I guess they are. Tomorrow, it is then. But it won't be on a Rawlins coach,' Jack had decided. 'The supply wagon pulls out midday, we'll load on to that. No one's goin' to expect an iron-bound, payroll box among Navy Plug an' long-johns.'

Jack looked hard at the bewildered group, his mouth slanted into a grim smile. 'I'll ride our coach in the mornin' as usual, but there'll be nothin' o' value in the boot, 'cept my boots.'

Owen Treebucks considered the plan for a moment. 'Hmm, sailin' under false colours, eh. It could work,' he said slowly. 'Who's ridin' guard with the supply wagon?'

Jack shook his head. 'No one. Be like holdin' up a playbill. Besides, who rides shotgun for miner's doodads? No, there'll be no guard!'

'So, it's simply *you* settin' yourself up for a bullet?' Rachel asked anxiously.

'That's what I've negotiated an' won five per cent for. Important thing is, they ain't gettin' more'n the ol' iron pot.'

'An' that's probably what they'll shoot you for.' Rachel turned to look at Treebucks, as if to influence her concerns.

'Well, Mr Treebucks,' Ralph wanted to know. 'If that's the way it's set up, you with us or Puggs?' he asked.

'I ain't a body for takin' chances,' Treebucks admitted. 'The Leesburg owners are though, if it's on someone else's time. So I guess we'll do it Harrow's way.'

It was the decision that Ralph wanted to hear, to make him feel a semblance of control again. 'I'll get Meeling to arrange things for first light,' he said.

A moment later the little group broke up. Jack was the first to leave. He picked up his hat from the hallway, had the door open when Rachel called after him.

'I didn't hear anyone sayin' thank you,' she said quietly.

Jack smiled. 'No. Sign o' the times, I guess. Anyway, you don't have to thank me. I got personal reasons...'

'The ones to make you stop by?'

Jack retained the smile. 'Might be.'

'Ralph didn't say much, did he?' Rachel said, after a moment's thought. 'You'd think he'd see that your way keeps the business, an' show *some* gratitude. I'm sorry for that.'

'I already said, it weren't him that brought me this way tonight. An' there's plenty of other business to for him to deal with ... where the water's cooler.'

Rachel nodded patiently, returned Jack's smile. 'An' I still haven't thanked you, have I?' she said, with clear feeling.

But that was just as Treebucks came from the parlour. He hauled up short, an uncomfortable expression setting his face. Rachel took a quick step back, and Jack glanced at the other man, winked slyly and pulled the door open. 'Until the mornin',' he said.

Treebucks made some curious noises in his throat, and clapping on his hat, he sidled past them, out on to the porch.

'I fear we embarrassed him,' Rachel observed drily, as Treebucks walked the overgrown path.

'Yeah, maybe,' Jack observed doubtfully. 'Certainly would've withered him if he'd left any later.'

'You a dancin' man, Jack Harrow?' Rachel asked unexpectedly.

'Hah. Only when there's someone puttin' bullets 'tween my toes. Why'd you ask?'

'There's a dance on Saturday night. I'd like to go.'

Jack made a shocked face. 'I've been on more medicine blankets than dance floors. You don't think I got me enough trouble in the meantime?'

'I do, yes. But you're not bent on lettin' a lady down are you?'

Jack gave his second smile of the day. 'No, Rachel, I'm certainly not,' he said, the meaning not at all clear. 'But right now, I ain't fer givin' anythin' more to the long-tongues o' this town.'

16

RUN TO THE MINES

A chill came with the new morning, and wind that blew gritty dust about the town. Already aboard the coach, Jack sheltered his cigarette behind a cupped palm, watched the horses stamping restlessly in their traces.

Owen Treebucks and Parker Meeling were making their way from the mines office and, as usual, Meeling was carrying the reinforced cash-box. When they reached the coach, Jack leaned down, grabbed a holding ring and immediately cursed.

'You could've loaded it with some goddamn rocks,' he snorted. 'You want everyone to know we're ridin' dry?'

True to character, the clerk didn't answer back, just looked up with his dark, humourless eyes. There was something about Meeling's sullen unhelpfulness that urged Jack to kick him, to try and crack out a response. But the man turned away, and Jack booted the empty box alongside the shotgun and his slicker.

For the next few moments, Jack mulled over his plan, eking out the flaws, the margins for error and risk. An image of Hote Stuckley's crafty eyes flashing above the red and white plaid of a neckcloth snaked through his mind. I wonder if the old buzzard's guessin' at what I'm up to? he wondered. But any realization ended when Harvey Maud clambered aboard, unwound the reins from the brake lever.

'Too late now,' Jack said, aggravating Maud's already worried countenance. Then he set himself for the jolt of the team's pickup.

As the last of the town's buildings fell behind them, Maud settled back to the monotony of the run. It was only then that he took a sideways glance at Jack. He gave him a brief nod, a non-committal grunt, and then turned his attention straight back to the rumps of the running horses. Maud was understandably ill-at-ease, it was his first encounter with Jack since the hold-up. As a consequence of the trouble he'd caused through his broadcast suspicions, he didn't know what to expect from the silent, brooding man beside him. Similarly, Jack let the man's uneasiness fester away, as he watched the dirt road winding on ahead of them.

There was heavy cloud weighing down the sky above the distant timbered ridges. But Jack had a poncho, a wedge of cheese, an assortment of guns, and on the appearance of a scheduled run, they were set for Fishtrap's Leesburg mines.

It was when they were less than two miles out of Laurin Flats, that Jack saw the rider standing on the road ahead. The man lifted a hand, made no other movement as the coach bore down on him.

'It's Redland,' Maud said, placing his foot higher up the brake lever. 'What d'you suppose he wants?'

'No idea. Bet you thought for a moment it was one o' my wayward buddies, eh?' Jack asked sarcastically.

As the coach pitched to a halt, the sheriff kneed his horse close to the front wheel. 'I'm with you on this trip,' he announced, nodding at the guard and driver. 'Best you clear town, though.' He jerked his head toward the coach. 'Guess I'll make myself comfortable inside.'

Redland was riding a livery horse, a rim-rock mare that would return to its barn when set loose. He dismounted and bow-knotted the reins, gave the animal's dusty flank a smart slap. Then he climbed into the coach, his hard features twisting as he pulled himself up the iron steps. He'd barely time to seat himself before Maud once again set the team against their collars.

Jack was in two minds about this latest development. The sheriff had a reliable gun hand, would be capable help if and when the coach ran into trouble. But Jack had been thinking of settling up with Hote Stuckley without the interference of the law. Nevertheless, under the lowering sky, they rolled on through the grey morning. Jack remained deep in thought, looked keenly at the timberline as the ground eventually started to climb.

As the coach climbed higher, the upper peaks of the Beaverheads became lost in shifting streamers of fog, and fine rain needled out of the overcast. Jack hauled out his slicker, while Maud rumbled and scowled, hunched deeper into the collar of a heavy mackinaw.

They lifted into the tall, yellow pine and Jack's tension became ever more acute. In the crowding ranks of timber, he strained to see beyond the dark shadows where a man could pick his shot. 'Driver'll give you no trouble. Take the guard from his perch',

111

Ormer Pugg had said. Jack grunted his agreement. It was unquestionably the way he'd do it himself.

Ahead loomed the narrow, rocky draw that would take them toward the higher passes. Maud began to gather the lines, readied his brake for slowing the five-horse team. Beneath his slicker, Jack quietly loosened his Colt, but there was no movement from the surrounding timber.

The coach stopped, and Maud set the brake. He stretched his cramped limbs, used the wheel spokes in stepping to the ground. Still there was no sound, other than the bluster of the horses, the cluck of a troubled blue jay that faded back into the refuge of the hills. Close to the road side, the trees now stood dark and heavy with fog and drizzling rain.

Jack wasn't moving from his seat. He sat and wondered again about Hote Stuckley, his plans for the Fishtrap shipment. Strange thoughts went through his head, led him to weigh up the distances between Laurin Flats and the Leesburg mines. By the time Maud was back in his seat, he'd made up his mind.

'Let's get to Fishtrap,' he said. 'An' take us there quick.'

Maud wasn't going to ask any questions. 'I

will. But I ain't runnin' these ladies to their death,' he responded. 'They're the only team we got on this run.'

Scattered among the hills were more than a score of worked-out mines. One by one they'd closed, when either the minerals or the backing dried up. Fishtrap was no more promising than any of the other townships when it began its fevered life. It was where Leesburg had invested, and as such, it was still hanging on. Amongst the blowdown, false-fronted buildings and tents of all descriptions dotted the mountain slope, unsightly tailings and blackened mine shafts rose starkly to mark the camps.

The stagecoach from Laurin Flats came pitching in at the end of its fast run, gave rise to the excitement which attended its twice-weekly arrival. At the log station Jack was already climbing down before the iron brakeshoe took hold. An anxious-looking man in a dark suit confronted him.

'Where's the payroll?' he wanted to know. 'These are needy men, an' they're owed. You ain't goin' to tell me–'

'I ain't goin' to tell you nothin' until you stop rantin',' Jack interrupted the Leesburg paymaster. 'But we ain't got it with us, an'

113

there'll be an explanation later. Right now, I want someone to get me a horse.'

Without meeting the man's eye, Jack strode off. He was looking for the station boss. 'Get me one o' your saddle mounts. A good one,' he demanded.

'Two. Make that two,' the sheriff growled. Elmer Redland lumbered up, met Jack's questioning look. 'I'll just ride along with you, Jack. You ain't hit trouble yet ... must be about due.'

Jack knew he couldn't stop the lawman from doing whatever he wanted to do or from going wherever he wanted to go. He shrugged and turned away impatiently. 'Where the hell's them saddlers?' he rasped.

But the mounts were soon saddled and ready. His horse was a grey with the long, strong build of a pacer. Rachel kept good animal stock for Rawlins Haulage, and Jack was grateful for it. He didn't look to see if the sheriff was ready, pushed on through the gather of restless mine workers. He wondered why they weren't working, thought maybe it had something to do with not being paid. He headed down the steeply pitched and muddy street, but Redland was already up with him, his own grey gelding kicking up dollops of sticky mud.

'Nice day for ridin' circle,' he grunted, 'if you don't take a fall.'

Jack said nothing, reined the grey in a little. There was a distance to cover and he wanted no mishaps.

As they dropped away from the unsightly mining town, met the first ranks of timber, he figured on the likely speed of the approaching supply wagon. Considering the time it was leaving Laurin Flats, they'd be doing well to meet it much before it negotiated the pass.

'Jack? You goin' to tell me what this is all about?' Redland asked after a while. 'An' where the hell we're goin' in such a hurry?'

'You're the one decided to come along,' Jack responded, not relaxing his irritation at the sheriff being there. 'Like me, you'll find out when we get there.'

17

BURNED GOODS

The rain had come and gone, though Jack had left his poncho in the boot of the coach, with the shotgun. There were no scabbards on their saddles, and Redland had tied his Winchester by his saddle strings. They were riding light, made good time through the timber. It seemed to Jack that time was unmoving in the gloom of the tall pine, where heavy cloud still obscured the westering sun.

When they began to climb higher toward the pass, Jack looked ahead for a sign of the supply wagon. In his estimation, it should have got that far since its scheduled departure from Laurin Flats. But when the two riders stopped to let their horses blow, there was no sight or sound of the Rawlins vehicle.

Jack compassed the eastern slopes, the dark mantling of timber, that was now partly obscured by streamers of pale cloud. Redland did the same, then his attention settled on Jack. 'Well?' he said. No doubt to a meaning.

'It ain't quite what I expected. But if it's trouble, it's about due. You said so yourself, Sheriff.' Then, turning to his horse, Jack adjusted a cinch before swinging back into the saddle.

The two men rode on, down from the pass, to the switchback where the trees again rose to surround them. Jack knew there could be other reasons for not having met the supply wagon; a breakdown, a horse going lame, a delay on starting – though not one of them likely. Now, grim presentiment took hold of his mind, settled across his tight shoulders. He knew what they were going to find around one of the approaching bends in the timber-choked road, felt his stomach churn when he saw it.

At the edge of the road, the Rawlins supply wagon was pulled over sharply, collapsed on its rear axle. The tang of charred timbers cleaved the air, grew sharper as the riders heeled the horses forward.

One of the lead team had been dropped by a bullet, a knife had been used to slash the other horses free from their traces. Someone had attempted unsuccessfully to fire the wagon. The red-painted Rawlins sign was blistered, and the canvas was hanging in charred shreds. But the wagon box was built solid enough to remain intact.

Redland shifted uneasily. 'You see the driver?' he muttered, climbing down from the saddle. 'Yeah, I see him,' Jack said, looked down at the boots that poked out from the offside of the wagon.

Jack dismounted, dropped the reins and went to take a closer look at the man lying face down in the hard dirt. He knew him, he was George Bowdle, an occasional Rawlins teamster. Redland kneeled, turned the man over. They saw the blood caking thin in the dust, the stained front of the hickory shirt where the bullet had broken his chest.

Bowdle's Colt was less than a foot from his outstretched fingers. Redland picked it up and noticed the spent shell beneath the hammer, sniffed at the sour taint of the barrel.

'He took a shot at somethin'. Could've told his childer o' this, if he'd stayed his hand,' Redland said angrily.

'Maybe. Maybe not,' Jack answered back. 'Whoever did it, would have decided *that*.' He turned away, stepped on the rear wheel hub, and swung up for a look into the body of the wagon. It was a tumbled mess of burned boxes, bags and loose freight. A sack of candles had helped the burning spread through a carton of scarves, gloves and beaver hats. Jack knew there was no use turning the goods over in the hope of finding the Leesburg payroll. It wasn't going to be there.

He jumped down, looked squarely at Redland. 'You've guessed it, Sheriff. The mine cash was *here*. We rode the coach with an empty box.'

Redland nodded. 'I guessed it back at Fishtrap. You said as much to the puffy suit. What I don't know is, whose idea was it?'

'Mine.'

'Yeah ... chose the right smart word there.' Redland moved away a pace, and back again, his hard features even tighter. 'One man did this,' he said. 'The tracks are plain to see. One man, an' he makes a fool of us all.'

'We been duped sure enough, but you can leave yourself out of it, Sheriff. You been nothin' more'n a witness.'

'Yeah, but *you* ain't, Jack,' Redland muttered, an impenetrable trace in his voice.

'They didn't need to send more one of 'em,' Jack said, ignoring Redland's remark. 'It was a set-up. Bowdle weren't goin' to give 'em trouble.'

119

'No. Doubt he ever shot more'n a barkin' squirrel.' Redland sniffed forcefully. 'Nothin' much more we can do here. Seems hardly worth it, but I expect Rawlins'll send up a salvage cart. We'll put Bowdle in the wagon, then I'll have a look around. Sign can't be more'n two hours old. Hard to follow though, in this thick-skinned country.'

Bowdle weighed little, and they got him up and into the wagon easily enough. Jack broke open a new blanket coat to cover him with. 'Company bequest. He earned it,' he said. 'An' I'd like to know where he put that bullet.'

Seated on the grey again, Jack looked at Redland who was slowly poking a toe into the stirrup of his own saddle. 'So long, Sheriff,' he called out. 'This time I *am* goin' alone.'

Redland removed his foot, stood with a fist around the saddle horn. 'Goddamn it, Jack. You an' me got a heap o' straight talkin' to get through. This mess is mostly down to you, I'm thinkin'.'

'Not quite, Sheriff. But now I've got a fair idea *who*. An' if you follow me this time, I swear I'll bring you back an' lay you down by ol' Bowdle there.'

With his threat ringing in Redland's ears,

Jack jogged the grey away from the wagon. He didn't doubt he'd hear plenty later. Redland would be a dangerous man to cross, let alone make threats to.

When he'd covered a mile or so, he turned off the stage road and struck into the timber. He worked higher, threaded a way among the tightly stacked pine. Damp hung in the needles of the branches, made the underfoot duff spongy and slick. But Jack took an unswerving course, disregarded the shivery chill that cut through his clothing.

In the failing light of first dark, he was tucked into the shelter of an aspen stand. He looked down on the abandoned mine and its ramshackle buildings. No movement stirred the stillness of the barren slopes, and no candle burned yellow from behind the cabin's dingy window.

As he'd done a few days before, Jack dismounted. Holding the bridle reins loosely, he walked his grey towards the cabin. He didn't touch his guns; this time he was completely alone.

He kicked open the squealing door, took it half off its rusted hinges. In the bleak half-darkness, he saw the cracked stove and the disordered bunks. Rain water seeped from a tear in the low overhead canvas. On top of the clutch of Wanted posters, Jack saw the folded sheet of paper with his name scrawled large. He toe'd away an upturned crate, pulled the paper from its nail, and took it closer to the open doorway. He read the message and, as he did so, the image of Hote Stuckley floated up at him from the words:

Figured you'd show, Jack. You looking out for them greenbacks sounds like the duck leading the fox away from her chicks. Nice try – but I know otherwise. Can't risk staying for another pow-wow – you're too good for that. Hope the old wagon jehu don't play the hero and give me trouble. Don't come looking. I got me a real neat hidey-hole.
H.S.

'At least we know why you shot him,' Jack muttered, read one of the lines again, before screwing up the note.

Although he and Hote Stuckley had taken different routes, there were many memories still holding them together. And Jack knew the inevitability of them meeting, despite Stuckley's self-imposed hiding. Jack cursed and left the cabin, wearily climbed back into the saddle. He took a last glance at the desolate country around him, heeled the grey back to the road, and Laurin Flats. That was something else to look forward to, meeting up with the Ralph and Rachel Rawlins. He wondered if there was any chance of *them* going into hiding.

Not five minutes after empty silence returned to the abandoned workings, another rider emerged from the aspens. Sheriff Elmer Redland picked his way cautiously down the uneven slope toward the ruined buildings. He reined in, sat in the dusk for a long moment considering his thoughts. He took off his hat and scratched the top of his grizzled head. 'Just ain't no one to tell me what the hell's goin' on,' the man rumbled.

18

UP AT THE HOUSE

Jack was on his way to the Rawlins' house. It was late, but there was still a light in the office of the haulage company as he rode past. He dismounted and hitched the grey, stood a moment in the chill darkness, prepared himself for a reunion somewhat earlier than expected.

Ralph was sitting in the inner office where a smaller lamp burned. He was sitting at Rachel's desk, his elbows propped, his head dropped in his hands. He raised a tired face when Jack pushed through the door.

'You look like you know somethin',' Jack said in anticipation.

Ralph nodded. 'We had a rider ... came straight from Fishtrap. Someone ... somehow got word. We've already sent up for George Bowdle's body. Maybe there's some other stuff we can bring back ... I don't know.'

Jack removed his hat, tossed it onto the

bench inside the door. He pulled the flat of his hand across his mouth, looked at the smear of dust. 'If only you could have your time over again, eh Ralph,' he said.

Ralph shrugged. 'That's for fools ain't it? If you're talkin' personal, best forget it. I approved what we wanted to approve. I'm as much to blame as anyone else.'

Ralph spoke unmovingly, but there was something in his manner that interested Jack, make him wish there'd been a scribe present, to get the words exact. This wasn't what he'd expected. He thought that Ralph would have jumped at the chance to heap the blame on to someone else.

Jack got to thinking that maybe Ralph did have some guts, a sense of fair dealing to go with it. All it took was a line of trouble to bring it out.

'What's Treebucks got to say? Has he heard?' he asked.

Ralph nodded. 'Yeah, he's heard. He was here less than an hour ago. Ormer Pugg worked him over. Didn't have to use his fists either. So all the Leesburg business is switchin' to Pugg's new company at the end o' the month.'

'I don't suppose it would've done any good to tell him that Pugg's the one who's behind all our troubles?' Jack suggested. 'I mean, what else has he been workin' for?'

Ralph shot him a close look. 'You think Pugg set this up?'

'Knew it first off. I had a head start, don't forget ... knowin' it wasn't me.'

'But there's nothin' you can prove.'

'Yeah, I know that too.' Jack thought for a moment. 'So what the hell happens next?'

Ralph pushed back from the desk. 'That's not hard to figure. The Leesburg account's our mainstay. Losin' it cripples us. The others'll dip out, go where Treebucks goes.' A humourless smile creased the man's weary face. 'With the way I've been thinkin' recently, this is just a quick way o' finishin' me off.'

'You can climb down, Ralph. That guilt stuff don't work on me. There'll be other customers, an' you still got a sister who'll stick with you. That's a veritable army with me on board. I'm thinkin' your pa should've taken more trouble to prepare you. Like mine, he weren't goin' to live forever. I think you're owed another year, Ralph.'

'I don't want another goddamn year,' Ralph decided vigorously. 'I'm through.'

Jack shrugged and went for his hat. 'I guess that's *it*, then. There's nothin' more I can do.'

Ralph got to his feet, scraped the chair legs across the floor. 'I'm sorry for the trouble between me an' you, Jack,' he said. 'I'll have Parker settle your pay first thing tomorrow.'

'Thanks. I'll drop by sometime to pick it up.' Jack turned, was about to leave when he hesitated. 'Parker Meeling? Where's he stand with you?' he asked unexpectedly.

'Huh?' Ralph was a little surprised. 'Don't really know, just that he does. He's not the sort to wear it on his sleeve, but he's about as loyal as you'd get. Why'd you ask?'

'I was just thinkin'. You know, picketin' them that get to carry on livin'.'

For all Ralph's resolution, Jack knew he wasn't yet through with the Rawlins. He could walk away from Ralph, but not Rachel, although he hadn't seen or heard from her since Treebucks disrupted their moment of near intimacy at the family house.

Standing outside of the haulage office, Jack brushed at the front of his pants, smoothed his hair and replaced his hat, tugged firmly at the brim, before setting a path to the Rawlins' house.

Rachel opened the front door to his knock, and as the light spilled onto the porch he stood for a moment staring. You're dressed up for a dance that I ain't taking you to, he thought to himself.

'You'll catch all the buckeyes in Montana with that mouth,' she said with a broad smile.

'Huh? Oh sorry, Rachel. Just recently, I ain't seen much that's as easy on the eye,' he said, with his own retiring smile.

'I usually get into these duds in the evenin'. It's an old custom. Pa always had us dress for dinner.'

Jack removed his hat, didn't know if he was getting the truth or not.

'If it's some sort o' business meetin' you're after,' she said, 'you can come in ... take a nightcap.'

Jack took a seat in the parlour while Rachel poured him a big glass of brandy. It would have been from her brother's supply, from a depleted decanter that sat atop an enormous mahogany sideboard.

'Thanks, Rachel. Been bad has it?' he asked.

'What do *you* think, Jack? Watchin' everythin' crumble, watchin' it go. This house'll be next, peelin' paint an' all. Our customers off lickety-split to Pugg's new outfit. An' Ralph, well he's–'

'In a mighty melancholic kind o' mood,' Jack interrupted. 'I just seen him in the office. He's sayin' his hand's folded, but there's somethin' else, an' I can't put a finger on it.'

Rachel set the heavy decanter on the table beside her. 'I'd like to know what he's got in mind ... what he's likely to do next,' she said, her shoulders lifting and falling.

'Well, whatever it is, Rachel, he's doin' it without me. This time I'm bein' paid off.' Jack finished his drink, put down the empty glass. 'I regret you lost the Treebucks account, an' no mistake,' he declared.

'Too late for regrets, Jack, an' I'm sure you'd have told Ralph the same thing,' she retorted. 'No, they were determined to break us, an' they reckon they have.'

Rachel poured more brandy into Jack's glass. But then she quickly picked it up and gulped it down herself. She pulled a bitter face, made a long sucking noise. Almost immediately the colour flushed her cheeks.

'But what the hell do *they* know?' she challenged thickly.

Jack gave a short laugh. 'Your brother seems to think that havin' your time over is for fools. But if you *could*, would you go for makin' your business work out, or would you walk away?' he responded, untroubled by Rachel's behaviour.

'Ralph might think he's finished, but I'm not goin' to be beat by the likes of Ormer Pugg.' The Rawlins girl smiled again, but it didn't touch her eyes.

'Good,' Jack said. 'I don't aim to be beat by him either. An' what's more, I can engage myself without the burden o' bein' paid for it.'

19

FIGHTING TALK

Under the overhead lamps outside of Humble's mercantile store, Nell Yuman stopped to check her store boughts. When Jack approached, she gave him a stony look. 'Goin' to invite me back to your room? Or ain't it dark enough yet?' she mocked.

Jack took a deep breath. 'If you believe that o' me, it don't say a lot for the way your mind works, Nell. I'd never get to think anythin' like that o' *you*,' he responded calmly.

'I'd never give you goddamn cause to, Jack Harrow.'

Jack shook his head disappointedly. 'What is it with the ladies o' this town? Of a sudden, they sound as if they're bitin' for lead steer. Got the attitude, too.'

'You suggestin' I'm, I'm...?' Nell, started indignantly. 'Don't you dare talk–'

Jack held up his hand. 'I'm sayin' you're to hold up with your fanciful observations.

Rachel Rawlins is a business partner. Sometimes, a business appointment's got to fall outside o' regular office hours.'

Nell's jaw dropped with incredulity. She was about to respond, give something about her good sense, when she noticed Ormer Pugg approaching quickly from the direction of the livery.

Pugg stepped directly up on to the walkway. 'You in trouble, Miss Yuman? Somethin' I can help you with?' he asked unctuously.

Nell glanced slyly at Jack, before answering. 'Nothin' I can't handle, Mr Pugg,' she said.

Pugg's eyes narrowed. 'Sorry,' he responded, turning to face Jack as he spoke. 'From way down the street, it looked like you weren't too happy at this exchange o' words.'

'Either way, it weren't none o' your business,' Jack sneered his opinion. He got near to a smile for Nell. 'An' now, if you'll excuse me, ma'am, it's gettin' late an' I need some grub.'

The nerve under Jack's left eye twitched as he tugged at the brim of his hat. His hand hid the quick few words he had for Pugg. 'You come bustin' into my hole once too often, Pugg. Stay away.' Jack started towards the boarding-house, hopeful of shaking the man off. 'Leave me be, Pugg, I'm tellin' you,' he said, the words trailing back over his shoulder.

But Pugg was following on. 'We got some unfinished business, Harrow. An' delays have dangerous ends,' he threatened.

Jack didn't respond. He kept going until he stood outside of McRae's Boarding-House. 'If this is the place, you'll be swingin' while I'm suppin',' Jack shot back, as he went through the door that led to the dining-room.

Less than ten feet away, the ample figure of Precious McRae sided between two tables. She looked up and smiled, placed a gravy boat beside a customer's empty plate.

'If you got an' out-o'-the-way corner table...?' Jack asked. 'I got a friend joinin' me.'

'You ain't hidin' behind skirts or fixins', Harrow,' Pugg said, as he now close-targetted Jack. The impending threat was obvious in his looming stance, the set of his shoulders.

Jack groaned his regret, looked ruefully to Precious. 'There'll be some clearin' up this night,' he said. 'My friend's changed his mind ... he's for takin' me apart.'

Resignedly, he lunged forward, his fist on

133

track for Pugg's jaw. He felt the stabbing jolt as he connected, but having pushed for the fight, Pugg knew it was coming. Before Jack could get balanced, a retaliating blow landed solid behind his ear, rocked him further forward. His head exploded with sharp pain, but it was what he needed. It cleared away the emotion, returned sharp thoughts. When Pugg followed with a short, chopping drive, Jack was already moving. He blocked the punch, gave a muscled uppercut in return.

Pugg took the blow, but slipped awkwardly on the polished floor. He went down, the momentum carrying him through into the dining-room proper. A couple of ladies shrieked as he spun himself around, scrambling for a way back. He clawed at a table, brought plates, eating utensils and a water jug crashing to the floor. His coat flapped open, and Jack grunted in satisfaction at sighting no gun. He pressed forward, waited for Pugg to get back on his feet.

Pugg was up and charging straight at Jack. Their fists met, arms parried and heads bruised in clashing, as they slugged some more. Pugg didn't carry the disposition of a hard man, but he was tough, had got resolve and a score to settle. He wasn't for letting Jack best him a second time.

The combatants fought their way backwards and forwards across the dining-room, pushing away tables, kicking at chairs. The few remaining customers had taken to the corners of the room, were watching with frozen fascination.

'Someone put a stop to this,' one of the ladies yelled. 'Go fetch the sheriff.'

Now Jack was distracted for a moment, lost his balance on the wet-slick floor. He doubled over while taking a hammer blow on the back of his neck. He blinked against the bright sparks, a moment later sent Pugg sprawling backwards into the doorway. Pugg swung around, caught a handful of swagged curtain as he went to his knees.

Jack waded straight in as Pugg got to his feet, squared to met him. Both men now had blood smeared across their taut faces, and their clothes were sagged and sweaty. They fought across the lobby, until Jack was found with his back against the reception desk.

'Get two tickets for Miles City ... an' a date for leavin',' he gasped at Precious, who'd followed them through from the dining-room. 'I ain't puttin' up with this town much longer.'

Pugg's hands shot out, grabbed for Jack's

throat, his panting breath hot and foul across Jack's face. For a moment, Jack thought he couldn't break free. Pugg's fingers tightened like steel rail dogs. Jack was fighting for air as he swung in a chopping hand to the side of Pugg's head. Pugg staggered, and Jack caught him with the same blow again.

But the last few days' events were coming to bear, and Jack was tiring fast. His legs started to give at the knees, his fists making more glancing contact. He wanted a final drive into Pugg, had levered his arm back, when someone stepped forward and made a grab for him.

'For God's sake, stop. You tryin' to kill each other?' This time it was a man's voice that rived the pounding atmosphere.

Jack was thinking that that they'd both been well on the way, when, Pugg connected with a crushing blow to the side of his head. He went down, but came to almost immediately he hit the floor. From the level of legs and assorted footwear, he raised his chin, spat drily and looked out for Pugg.

But his adversary had made up his mind. *He* wasn't there until the death. The moment Jack fell, he used his remaining judgement and reeled for the way out.

Jack grunted, and scrambled back to standing, made his way through the retreating mill of shocked onlookers. He made some offensive remarks, settled a bit when he saw the wetness of Precious McRae's eyes.

'I'm real sorry, Precious,' he said, with genuine and intimate concern. 'I swear that won't ever happen again.'

He elbowed his way outside, walked along the side of the building to where the steps led up to his old room. He leaned against the wall, made an unconvincing start for his cigarette makings. He drew a fingertip across his teeth, looked distractedly at the smear of blood. Where the hell's Pugg gone? he wondered. What the hell's wrong with the man? Presumably, he'd got what he wanted with the breaking of Rawlins Haulage. He didn't need public conflict, a fist fight. But if he *did*, that's what it was mostly about – personal compensation. For a business man, that really didn't make much sense, Jack decided.

He gave up the speculating and lifted his head shakily, stared blearily around as an awareness of his surroundings returned. He dully remembered that the sheriff had been sent for, but right now, he wasn't for mixing Elmer Redland's law business with his social life. He pushed away from the wall of the building, and turned back to the door of the boarding-house, watched with drained amusement as one or two watchers drew quickly back inside.

But he didn't follow them. Instead, he made off into the night. The bracing coolness brushed at his sweat, helped erase some of the tired fogginess from his head. By the time he'd got to the Rawlins' house at the edge of town, he was feeling a little better, although there was a profound weariness in his step.

The light was on in the hall when Jack pulled the bell cord. But there was no movement through the window glass, and after a moment's wait he turned away. He couldn't be certain about Ralph, but Rachel would have been in. He'd even got an opening of sorts. 'Don't suppose I'm in the frame for a wash an' brush up?' was going to be his irresistible starter.

Now, uncaring, and with a curious feeling of relief, he went back down the weed-grown path, turned left and headed towards the stable to collect his gelding. 'Should never have come back into town,' he muttered. He swore at the Rawlinses and about working for anyone other than himself. 'Yeah, should never have come back to goddamn fence-makin' either.' Maybe ... just maybe, he thought, that right now was the time to settle down with a contented wife, a cosy store-keeper's job. And, of course, there would always be the alternative of going back to the old ways, doing what he was actually good at.

20

DEADLY COMPANY

In a wide, narrow room that ran across the rear of the new stage-line building, Ormer Pugg stared into the darkness. Suffering from the beating that Jack Harrow had meted out, he wasn't entirely sure how he'd got back. He groaned, and twisted over on the damp-sweat bedclothes. He wondered why he'd allowed himself to get into such a shameful brawl, why he'd goaded a man who was so hard to beat. He knew there'd be an upshot, but not from Harrow: more from the man whose money actually bankrolled the work he was meant to be doing in Laurin Flats.

The unpromising thought dragged him up off the low cot, sent him stumbling to find a lamp and get it burning. His temporary quarters smelled of raw lumber, turpentine and paint from the refurbished building and coach painting. He squinted at his reflection in the small mirror that was propped above the washstand and basin, and cursed painfully. He looked at the bleeding knuckles of his right hand, felt where all the teeth of one side of his jaw ached. He cursed, wondered if he'd inflicted comparable damage on Jack Harrow.

His muscles hurt, as he pulled off his ripped clothing and threw them to the floor. He removed his shirt and soaked it in water from a jug, tentatively rubbed his body in an attempt to clean up. His head was down; it was as he looked up that he glanced again at the mirror, noticed the shadowy figure of his visitor.

Rachel Rawlins had managed to enter the room quietly, stood with her back and shoulders pressed to the closed door. She said nothing, the silence running, as Pugg stared, bemused.

'I really weren't expectin' company,' he said after a long shaky moment. 'You come to see what Harrow did?' Pugg waited again before asking, 'Or you just findin' it real hard to stay away from men's rooms?'

'Real smart. But I can see how someone might think that,' Rachel retorted, in little more than a strangled whisper. Then, in a white-knuckled grip, she raised the gun that she'd been holding at her side; it wavered, gleamed in the yellow lampglow.

Pugg looked at it, his face bruised and blank. 'You ain't goin' to bring much down with that, lady,' he said shortly. 'An' you ain't got the nerve.'

'You've wrecked our livelihoods, Pugg. Me an' Ralph ... all we had,' Rachel came back. 'Killin' you's goin' to be no more difficult than stompin' a roach.' Rachel smiled cold and calculating as she levelled her pa's old pistol at Pugg. 'If you're thinkin' I ain't likely to hit your gut with this defective piece o' junk, ask yourself, could this be one o' them cruel times when all six barrels go off at once?'

Now, with a trace more emotion, Pugg looked at the gun, saw the hammer lift under the pressure of Rachel's finger. He raised a hand in restraint. 'OK,' he started, 'I've made some mistakes here. Gettin' killed would be the big one. Don't leave time to get much put right.'

'An' how'd you even start that?'

'Tellin' the truth?' Pugg suggested. 'Could be why I got so upset at Harrow – a man with hard fists and a yen for gun work, but just about every girl in town lookin' out for him.'

'So, how does the truth figure in that observation?'

142

'It's me. I fell for you, Rachel. Didn't reckon on that.'

'You're tellin' me that's it? It ain't *business* that's bitin' your butt? You went for Harrow 'cause o' *me?*'

'Yeah, that's about it,' Pugg owned up.

Rachel nodded, for a moment, uncertain of the new ground. 'Well you sure messed up,' she decided. 'The business is gone ... an' your chances o' me, along with it.'

'But it ain't final,' Pugg returned with an eager edge.

'What're you talkin' about?'

'I can put things right ... still. I can finger who's hirin' me for this job. It gets me a stretch o' can time, but you an' your brother get the business back.'

'An' you'll do this for...?' Rachel wanted to know.

'For ... well, I don't have to spell that out, do I, Rachel? I'm askin' for a chance ... later on. I got to be sure though. You're the only thing that makes it worthwhile.' Of a sudden, Pugg's voice went hard, an intense look burned into Rachel's face.

Rachel too discovered a strange, new emotion; a perverse fascination for the man who stood before her. 'To save our company, I'll consider most offers,' she said. 'Truth be told, you ain't the worst flusher that ever come my way. You save us, an' me an' Ralph will see to it that you don't get to any prison.' With that, Rachel lowered the pepperbox and Pugg took a deep breath.

The relief was still easing across his face, when the startling smash of a gunshot filled the open window with flame and noise. Rachel watched petrified as Pugg's breath exploded from his lungs and his dead weight crashed towards her. From the pounding of the bullet in the middle of his back, he went down to his knees. Rachel staggered back, drew in her hands and dropped the unfired pistol. She saw the blood, gulped down a horror-struck scream when Pugg's face smacked into the floor.

Within a matter of seconds, someone was running excitedly between the livery and the shed, shouting, calling out for the source of the gunshot. Rachel stood unmoving beside Pugg's body. She couldn't have called for help, even if her numbed brain had wanted her to.

'Here, Sheriff,' a voice yelled. 'Back o' the sheds.'

More running feet sounded dully, and then the door was thrown open under the heavy hand of Elmer Redland. The sheriff had arrived with three or four men crowding his back. He ran his keen glance across the room, missed nothing. 'Stay out,' he shouted to those outside, then he entered the room. His jaw ground tight with estimation as his eyes moved from Pugg's body up to Rachel. 'Jack Harrow been here, has he?' he asked, with a distinct narrowing of his eyes.

Other than a slight shake of her head, Rachel didn't respond, didn't take her eyes from Pugg's body.

Redland lifted Rachel's handgun from the floor, took in the fact that it hadn't been fired. 'Did you see anythin', Rachel ... through the window?'

But Rachel wasn't going to answer and he turned back to the doorway.

'Stay away from that window,' he snapped. 'If there's any footprints, they'll be scoured by now, goddamnit.' He looked back to Rachel, took off his hat and scratched his grizzled head. 'What the hell happened, Rachel?' he persisted. 'It's plain as day somethin' did. Silence ain't always the safest way.'

'What you see's what happened. We were talkin', someone shot, he fell.'

Redland held up the gun. 'This curio belonged to your pa. So what the hell were you talkin' about?' he demanded.

'Nothin' to do with him gettin' shot.'

'I'll be the judge o' that, Rachel,' Redland said with a mild gruffness. 'But you're goin' to have to come up with somethin' sometime. This is Pugg's room, don't forget. So what you were doin' here – let alone talkin' about's one big hell of an interest to the law. Just tell me. I ain't goin' to use it against you.'

Rachel looked concerned, but she didn't speak, wasn't going to lie.

'Sheriff, get yourself out here. We got somethin',' a man suddenly shouted.

The sheriff gave Rachel another serious look, then he shrugged sadly, turned to consider the new development.

21

RAWLINS YARD

Redland strode outside, saw three men struggling towards him. In the poor light, he could see that one of them was being held, giving trouble in his efforts to break loose.

'What the hell's goin' on? Who you got there?' he demanded sharply.

'We found him hidin' out back o' livery,' one of the two restrainers said. 'He didn't want to come. Thought we'd better bring him though ... considerin'.'

Panting, Ralph Rawlins stood in front of Redland. His jacket was torn at the shoulder, his hair lank across his sallow face.

'What the hell you doin' out here, Ralph?' Redland asked in near disbelief. 'You totin' a gun?'

'No. An' I'll talk to *you*, not this bunch o' clowns.'

'One or two o' you stay here,' Redland notified the men who'd gathered around him. 'Hold the door, don't let anyone near.

I won't be more'n a few minutes. An' one o' you get the doc up here, for Miss Rawlins. Then see she gets home.'

'I want to have a word with my sister,' Ralph said.

'Yeah I thought you might,' Redland answered. 'But I can't allow that, an' you know it. You're comin' with me.'

The young Rawlinses weren't exactly friends of the sheriff, as their pa had been, but they'd been acquaintances for many years. Without protest, Ralph went with him to the jailer's office above the cells. The building was dark, except for a single table-lamp where the deputy was reading a news-sheet. Redland sent him out of the room, braced himself against the rubbed-worn edge of the desk top.

'I want your story now, Ralph,' he told his prisoner. 'Don't leave too much of it out.'

Ralph reached a slim, trembling hand to his face. 'I followed Rachel. I was at the house when she came in. But she left soon. There was somethin' goin' on. I knew it ... with all that happenin'.'

Redland nodded. He didn't interrupt, let Ralph go on with his story.

'She'd taken Pa's old pepperbox. We kept it at home ... sometimes at the office. It sort o' went most places, like a talisman. But I knew she'd taken it. Wouldn't you've wondered why?'

Redland nodded again. 'Yeah, guess I would. So you followed her to Ormer Pugg's ... saw whoever it was shoot through the window?'

'Yeah, I saw whoever it was. It was too dark to see who it was, though. They just came around the corner ... direction o' the livery. I heard the noise, then they were gone.'

'Hmm. What did you do?' Redland asked.

'I ran, that's what. You think I was goin' to stay around? We weren't exactly close-buddies, me an' Pugg. Wouldn'ta looked too good.'

'No it wouldn't, Ralph. But tell me, how'd you know your sister weren't lyin' there dead?'

Ralph grimaced. 'I didn't. It wouldn't have changed my position though.'

'That's true enough. Now tell me what Rachel an' Pugg were talkin' about. It's what you tailed her for. What was it, Ralph?'

'I don't know. I never got to hear ... didn't get to the window.'

Ralph was lying, Redland could see by the look of him, by the way he held his eye despite not wanting to. They'd reached a deadfall, and Redland knew it.

'I said not to leave too much out, Ralph. Now, you tell me the truth, or I won't be helpin' you.'

But Ralph didn't give any more, so Redland went to the door and called back the deputy. 'Give him a docket for anythin' he's got,' he said, tersely.

'What? You lockin' me up?' Ralph gasped.

'Sure am,' Redland acknowledged.

Minutes later, Ralph was secure in the cell that Jack Harrow had so recently occupied. Redland stood outside on the walkway, thinking on his next move. He sniffed the air, then hesitated and sniffed again.

The unmistakable tang of wood smoke tainted the crisp night air. He ran a sweeping look over the town, saw the bright, small sparks spurting upwards. Redland could all but hear the hiss and crackle of the distant fire, almost sense the affecting heat.

'It's Rawlins Haulage,' he breathed hollowly. 'In God's name, what more we got tonight?'

He started a heavy run toward the fire, joined with other folk now shouting their alarm. The steel triangle outside of Humble's Mercantile clanged its alarm into the darkness.

When he reached the yard, the main doors which were set in high board fencing had been already been dragged open. The place was seething with tension, the heat billowing, outlining the framework of the burning stock barn. He could feel the intense, fresh heat from the flames. Trapped horses were screaming, the thud of their frenzied hoofs carrying above the sounds of the fire and animated yelling. Men appeared through the gaping doors, their arms across their faces as they urged the fearful animals to safety.

Along one side of the fence, a freight wagon was ablaze. More men were struggling with it, dragging at the splinterbar, putting shoulders against the solid wheels. Redland joined in, fighting to roll the ponderous vehicle from the line to save two others.

Redland turned next to the stock barn, from where the last of the horses had been driven. A big dun had broken loose, was running wild about the yard, snorting its terror at the sight of fire which almost surrounded them all. Redland threw himself to one side as it stamped past him, watched it disperse another group to an accompaniment of shouts and warnings.

Someone called the sheriff's name and he turned. It was the Rawlins' clerk, Parker Meeling. The man's clothes were black with dirt and soot. He'd inhaled smoke, could hardly talk for a coughing spasm.

'Nearly a total loss,' Meeling rasped. 'We saved horses ... rollin' stock. Some feed's gone ... equipment.'

Lungs an' throat crispin' up, an' he says more now than in the previous couple o' years. Must be the vested interest, Redland almost said out loud. His thoughts were harsh, but mostly accurate. 'How'd it happen? You any idea?' he asked.

'Yeah, I got an idea. It's called fire-raisin' ... arson, I believe,' Meeling responded. 'Ask Peacepipe, that crazy old treaty Injun. Humble pays him a dollar to watch the town at night. He's sayin' he broke 'em up ... put a goddamn arrow into one of 'em. Have you seen Ralph?'

'Yeah, I seen him,' Redland said, after a moment. 'He's in one of our cells. Been in there most o' half an hour.'

'Half an hour ... what the hell's he–?' Meeling started, not understanding.

'I put him there 'cause he couldn't ... wouldn't give me good reason not to. Maybe he'll tell you what I want to know. Go talk to him. Say I said so.' Redland gave Meeling a penetrating look. 'The watchman,' he said. 'What else did he have to say about them torchers?'

'Nothin'. I told you, he's an Injun,' Meeling replied, already having started to turn away.

22

SHERIFF'S POSSE

Hote Stuckley was beginning to realize how badly he was hurt. He felt as though a fire filled his whole body, the running of his horse battering him with every hoofbeat.

He smelled the bloody sweat, felt the salt running into his eyes and, when he could take no more, he reined in. He held the reins in his mouth and clamped tight with his teeth. He squeezed the fingers of his right hand close to the wound, with the left quickly snapped the arrow. The point had locked into his hip bone, and the pain was so great, the trees and sky turned white, then silver then black with moons and shooting stars.

Sick and giddy he bent double for minutes on end, knew that if he'd dismounted he'd never have made it back up. He cursed the man who'd put an arrow in him, cursed the henchmen who'd scattered and left him on his own. He cursed the man who, panicky at the shortness of time, had ordered burning the stables as a final, frenzied effort to clinch Rawlins' downfall.

A terrible thirst was on him, his lips were dry but his face was bathed in sweat and he was shivering. He locked his knees to brace himself in the saddle, sent the horse forward again. He had to get help soon, and there was only one place he knew of. He squinted at the stars, tried to take a bearing.

After what seemed like endless hours of picking his way through sage and bunch grass, his horse stopped its arduous walk. Stuckley raised his head, saw the low, slanting roof of a logged building less than a hundred feet in front of him. To either side, he vaguely noticed open-fronted work-sheds with piles of fencing posts and bales of horse-nail barb wire. Further out was another building with log splitters, draw-files and sawhorses.

'Yeah, got to be it,' he muttered feverishly, at the yellow squares of house light. He eased his left leg from the stirrup, with an unbearable effort swung it across the back of the horse. His boot touched earth and the pain was too much to hold him.

He went down on hands and knees, remained there, hunched, as a pale wedge of light fell across him. The door of the house had opened and a man's figure showed dark in the threshold.

Stuckley fell on to his side, as he dragged his Colt from his holster. He looked to the light and blinked, tried to level the barrel as he heard the man approach him.

'What the hell you doin' here, Hote? What's wrong with you?' Jack Harrow asked.

Stuckley wanted to answer, but the words stuck somewhere between his brain and his mouth. A moment later, he was overwhelmed by impenetrable shadow.

Inside the house, still bruised and stiff from his encounter with Ormer Pugg, Jack worked on cleansing the wound which was deep in the flesh above Stuckley's hip. But he was lost in thought with his own predicament, didn't give much thought to what might have actually happened to Stuckley. He flinched when Stuckley regained consciousness, when the man's lips moved.

'It's bad ain't it?' Stuckley murmured. 'Got any drink? I wouldn't want to die from thirst.'

Jack swore and poured some whiskey. 'You ain't dyin',' he said, offering the tin cup to Stuckley's mouth. 'Now you can tell me why you been skewered. As if I really care.'

'Why'd you say that, Jack?' Stuckley answered, avoiding the nub of Jack's question.

'Because you got me euchred, an' ruined the prospects o' the people I work for. I was thinkin' o' movin' on. Maybe I should be thankin' you for makin' it easier.'

Stuckley coughed. 'That's for the best, Jack, an' you know it. You really spendin' the rest o' your life here? I just about seen your set up.'

'I would've liked the choice, Hote,' Jack suggested.

'Sorry. I got sucked in. It was the money he was offerin'. I couldn't resist.'

'Pugg offered you this money?'

Stuckley's features squeezed tight. 'No, not Pugg,' he wheezed. 'He was bein' paid, same as me. But I ain't goin' to tell you who, Jack. Us sort got reputations to keep.'

Jack slowly shook his head at Stuckley's obstinacy. 'You know why you don't see mules kickin' each other, Hote?' he said. 'Well I'll tell you: mutual respect. Anyways, you don't have to inform on anyone. I reckon I've known all the time. An' it's right sort o' pleasin', if you know what I mean.'

Stuckley moved his head into a slight nod of agreement, the hint of a smile. 'Who'da thought I'd get laid up by some skulkin' redskin carryin' a bow an' arrow?' Stuckley started a pained laugh. 'Where you movin' to, Jack? How's about me ridin' along ... like the old days?'

'If it was Peacepipe that shot you, I'm thinkin' the arrow head'll be made o' tin. So you'll probably be dyin' a slow death o' lockjaw or somethin', an' that'll just slow me down.'

Jack was accompanying Stuckley with a dark laugh, when they heard the footfalls of the approaching horse.

'Who the hell...?' Jack started, getting to his feet and moving fast to the door.

Nell Yuman was reining in her pony before the house. 'They're comin', Jack,' she called out breathlessly. 'Redland's got himself a posse, an' they're not far behind. You've got to ride, now.'

Jack stepped onto his narrow stoop, reached a hand towards the pony's bridle. 'Why should Redland be comin' out here?' he asked with obvious surprise. 'No one sends out a posse for fist fightin'?'

'I know nothin' about that, Jack. There were riders in the yard... Sheriff was talkin' to Pa. I heard 'em say your name ... couldn't hear much else. They're on the way here, though.'

'Yeah, you said, an' I thank you, Nell.'

'Please hurry, Jack. Is that your horse, still out front? It doesn't look fresh; you can take mine. I can draw 'em off. By the time they cotton on, you'll be into the Beaverheads.'

Jack was cut with a moment of indecision. 'You're gettin' yourself implicated, Nell. None of it's your problem, so why?'

'You mean, why am I here?' Nell's voice held the touch of exasperation. 'Just *because*, goddamnit,' she retorted. 'There'll be a time for tellin' you soon enough. But if you don't go now, we won't ever have that time. Is that a problem for you?' she demanded hotly.

Her answer came from the doorway. 'I'm the problem, lady. It's *me* they come for. An' that's my horse, not Jack's.' Hote Stuckley was slumping against the doorframe. His eyes desperate, wild and filled with pain.

Nell gasped. Her eyes flicked between the outlaw and Jack in search of an explanation.

'The man's right,' Jack supplied quickly. 'An' I'll tell *you* about it soon enough.' He smiled a short, but friendly smile, turned back to face Stuckley. 'Get back inside, Hote. I'm stayin'. This is my property, so I'll get rid of 'em.'

Uncomprehending, and now worried, Nell continued to stare.

Jack moved quickly, made a grab for

Stuckley. He reached for the man's pained body, pulled him back inside the house, towards the old davenport.

Stuckley saw his gun where Jack had placed it on a chair near the hearth, and he pushed Jack away, lurched forward. He clutched the Colt tight, turned it on Jack. 'You know I ain't goin' to use it, Jack, but right now, I'm delirious... a mite fickle,' he slurred. 'The lady's right, but it's for *me* to do the ridin'.'

Jack wasn't wearing a gun and his shoulders slumped at being foiled.

Stuckley grimaced. 'Thanks for the doctor-in',' he said. 'But don't go makin' a practice of it. So long.' With a fixed aim on Jack, he backed awkwardly through the door into the yard.

Nell Yuman had dismounted and she stood to one side, backed off from Stuckley. Then her attention was diverted, and she turned to face the shouts of the approaching horsemen.

23

RETURN TO TOWN

Hote Stuckley took a couple of shaky steps out towards where his horse was ground-hitched. But he knew his legs wouldn't hold him, and he cursed, swung back to face the posse. He cursed the world and his dog, lifted his Colt and fired steadily into the approaching horsemen. 'You'da done the same to me, fellers,' he reasoned.

Nell Yuman watched with dread as her pony crow-hopped away from the shooting, then she stepped into the house, saw Jack Harrow strapping on his own Colt.

Into the yard, Elmer Redland was shouting at his men. 'We want him alive. Control your fire.' But too many keyed-up men had drawn weapons, and the sheriff's warning was smothered under the roar of half-a-dozen guns.

Stuckley was a target too close to be missed, and he took most of the bullets. He jerked backwards, twisted half around under the intensity. Then he dropped, the dust eddying low around his sprawled body.

A heavy silence immediately mantled the yard. Then Redland was swinging down from his saddle, striding forward with some of the men crowding close. Others were sensing the wrong, and backing off.

From the doorway of the house, Jack turned and spoke quietly to Nell. 'Stay here ... keep out o' sight. It won't do any good for them to know you're here.' Then he, too, went to join the men who were staring down at Stuckley's body.

Redland hadn't recovered from his anger at the posse. 'Goddamned crock-heads,' he rumbled, glaring at the confused faces about him. 'What good's the man to us now? I wanted him to do some talkin'.' He shook his head crossly, realized there was no point.

'The man was hurt bad. He was dyin' on his feet ... so to speak,' Jack exaggerated. 'You wouldn't have got much talk out of him.'

'Ah yeah, Harrow,' Redland observed. 'I was just gettin' to wonder about you.' The light from the door fell across the small group of men as they gathered close. 'Perhaps what you got to say's good reason to have shot him dead,' the sheriff suggested.

Then, for what was almost becoming a habit, Jack hesitated. Hote Stuckley had settled for nothing in return by deciding to leave; except Jack's own life, that is. Quickly, Jack considered the truth and the lie, decided to split the difference.

'I can't tell you much,' he answered. 'Whoever he was, he tilled me from my bed ... made me clean up a goddamn arrow wound, of all things. A man carryin' the pain he'd got, weren't for arguin' with. He'd've shot me dead, an' that's for sure.'

Redland considered Jack's account. 'Well, we trailed him from town,' he said. 'Got near to the Yuman place. Nell's pa didn't know nothin' ... suggested he might have headed this way. An' you say you never seen him before?'

Jack shook his head. 'No, I never said that, Sheriff. But whether I have or haven't, what do *you* say?'

The sheriff weighed his words before he spoke. 'I ain't sure, Jack. I just don't know what to say or make o' you. There's been some bad things happening. An' when they do, you're plumb in the middle every time.' Redland took a lingering look at Jack, then nodded at Stuckley's body. 'Let's get this turkey's body onto a horse,' he directed

163

gruffly. 'There's nothin' more we can do here.'

'So what did he do to send you all out here?' Jack asked as the group broke up.

Redland sniffed, considered his answer. 'He set fire to Rawlins' wagon yard.'

The news struck at Jack like a hammer blow. He tried to separate the inner curses from the shock and concern. Jack knew that Stuckley had pulled off some really bad things in his life, but dying in a hail of lead was a high price to pay. He stood thinking for many minutes after the riders had gone, for as long as it took the dust to settle in his yard.

It was then that Jack realized that not all the riders had gone. One of them had stayed behind. In the lee of the cutting shed, a shadowy figure was standing very still.

'Where's Nell, Harrow? I know she's here.' Crawford Menroe called out with raw concern. Jack was still deep in thought. He recognized the voice, but didn't answer quickly.

Menroe pointed towards the far side of the yard. 'That's her pony,' he snapped. 'Tell me where she is, or there's goin' to be another killin' here.'

'You really are a miserable son-of-a-bitch, Menroe,' Jack struck back. 'I got a mind to let you try for it.' Then he turned, and called Nell from the house.

The weather-beaten old cowpuncher nodded when he saw Nell, stepped forward into the weak light. 'I come with the posse,' he explained. 'Never really reckoned to find you here.'

'She came to warn me about the posse,' Jack responded. 'That includes *you*, if you wish it.'

'Why else would I come here?' Nell furthered. 'You can trust me, Craw.'

'I do, missy,' Menroe answered back. 'Your pa's still got me lookin' out for you, so don't get mad.' Menroe directed his hostile stare at Jack again. 'That fight you had with Ormer Pugg?' he said. 'You come straight out here, or did you hang around a while?'

'Listen, mister,' Jack started impatiently. 'That town's one goddamn place I ain't ever hangin' around in. What's it matter to you?'

'It don't. I just wondered about Pugg gettin' himself shot dead ... the timin' of it.'

While Jack took everything in, all the implications, the likely suspects, Menroe continued, 'You see, I'm kind o' curious as to why Redland never made mention of it.'

Jack made a sneery, jaded smile. 'If I'd

wanted to kill Pugg, I'da done it at the time. What I wanted from Pugg, I got. I'm guessin' that even Redland reckoned on that. He's a shrewd of judge o' character, an' I'm warmin' to him. Unlike *you*, Menroe. Now make up your mind: you continuin' with this trespass or what?'

Menroe bristled at Jack's aggression. 'Why's Redland got Ralph Rawlins locked up? Answer me that, Harrow?'

Things were coming fast at Jack. He lifted a hand, pinched tight the corners of his eyes. 'I don't know … didn't know that,' he muttered tiredly. 'But maybe I owe him an' Laurin Flats one more visit. So as you're leavin', I'll ride with you.'

When he was ready to ride, Jack nudged his chestnut gelding alongside Nell's pony. 'There's folk who'll ask what you're doin' mixed up in all this, Nell. So I'd get yourself back home,' he said. 'I'm workin' on that promise o' meetin' up with you later.' Jack winked at the confidence.

Less than ten minutes later, the two men had their horses set into the darkness towards Laurin Flats. Menroe told Jack as much as he knew about the shooting of Pugg, the likely contributions of Rachel and Ralph Rawlins.

'Neither of 'em are sayin' much,' he said. 'But one of 'em's lyin' that's for sure.'

Jack listened with interest, then remarked that it was a longer, more darker night than normal.

'That's 'cause the sky's fillin' up with cloud. There's a big rain comin',' Menroe muttered.

Then they heeled their mounts, shortly noticed they were gaining on Redland and his posse.

24

CELL VISIT

It was near to three o'clock when they picked up the straggling lights of Laurin Flats. On a clear night, and given the opportunity, Menroe would have judged the hour by the configuration of the wheeling stars.

The clatter of Redland's returning posse brought townsfolk hurrying into the street in search of news. But the sheriff made a terse response. He thanked his riders for their help, then dismissed them. He asked one of them to knock up the undertaker, get Stuckley's body taken care of before morning.

Redland and Jack dismounted before the courthouse. Jack took a sideways glance at the street-level window of the cells, stepped onto the puncheoned walkway and into the office.

Barclay Kittle was on his way out, his manner puffy and contemptuous.

'I've been talkin' to your prisoner,' he

addressed the sheriff. 'Wouldn't surprise me if *he* was the man you're lookin' for. An' at this time o' night, your office will be gettin' a meat-filled tab.'

Redland gave him a dry look. 'You don't waste your time, do you?' he retorted. 'Innocence ain't much protection in your book, is it, Kit?'

The sheriff and Jack shoved past the old attorney, nodded at the deputy and stepped down the iron treads to the bleak cell corridor. Jack looked at the sign about tomorrow never coming, shuddered at the memory of the night he'd spent there.

Redland turned a key, pulled at one of the heavy wooden cell doors. Ralph Rawlins cut a sorry figure, bent forward with his arms wrapped around his knees. When he looked up from the narrow cot, his face was haggard, his eyes red-rimmed.

'You got yourself a visitor,' Redland announced summarily.

'What the hell do you want?' Ralph asked as Jack walked into his cell.

'To help you,' Jack said. 'Shoe was on the other foot the last time we hung around here, eh Ralph?'

The dry humour pulled at the corner of Ralph's bloodless mouth. 'Can't think what sort o' help that is?' he said. 'I'm the law's easy offerin'.'

Jack lowered himself onto the cot beside the prisoner, held out his tobacco pouch.

'I don't smoke,' Ralph said.

'I know,' Jack returned. 'But it's some way to what condemned men always ask for – apple pie an' cream, a girl o' the line, an' a store-bought smoke.'

Jack tried an encouraging smile. 'There's plenty we can do, Ralph,' he said calmly, and went about building himself a cigarette. 'If we can find out who shot Ormer Pugg, we can get you out o' this hell hole. All you got to do is tell me what it was you heard ... before the shot.'

'An' then I won't need that pie, eh?' Ralph looked up, returned a slight smile. 'OK,' he said, 'it's to do with Rachel.'

'Yeah, I know that, Ralph. She was with Pugg.'

'No, you don't understand,' Ralph said. 'Have you got feelin's for her, Jack?'

Jack lifted his head, turned a long, narrow look on Ralph. 'I'm not sure.' He wanted to say he'd got irons in the fire, but in the circumstances, thought it unproductive. 'There's a lot goin' on just now, Ralph. Ain't got time to get my feelin's into roundup. But

170

it don't lessen the responsibility I feel towards her, or you, for that matter. So what line are we all workin' on?'

'You're too good for her, Jack. Even a man like *you* deserves better.' Ralph's voice was suddenly strained with repressed emotion.

Jack shook his head for a moment of clarity, then he looked around him, as if for anyone listening. 'That's kind o' strong, Ralph, since I know what you think o' me,' he said. 'So, what the hell's Rachel done to deserve all this? Is it somethin' to do with what you heard?'

'Yeah. But I had to stop listenin'. I...'

'What? What did you hear, Ralph? Tell me, I really ain't got the time.'

'She was tellin' him that she was stayin' fresh with you, to keep you agreeable.'

At Ralph's disclosure, the muscle high on Jack's cheek started its nervy flicker. He knew he was being told how it was, but he wasn't going to break up over it.

'So, you reckon me an' Pugg were gulled?' he responded. 'Rachel was usin' him, too?'

'Yeah,' Ralph agreed thoughtfully.

'Gettin' him to talk? Givin' her a name, maybe?'

'Yeah. That was what I guessed might've happened.' Jack got to his feet, ground up

171

the remainder of his cigarette with his heel. 'There's only one way to find out. I'll just have to go an' ask her, see if she confirms my thinkin'. Don't get to prove much though.'

Before Ralph could say any more, Jack was walking away.

Elmer Redland had been waiting in the empty adjoining cell. He joined up with Jack in the corridor.

'You heard all that?' Jack asked him.

'O' course. So you got your own ideas, eh, Jack?'

'You know as much as I do, Sheriff. You just ain't added it up the same.'

'Huh, that's as maybe. Maybe my strength's in other areas,' Redland said unsurely. 'At least you got him to talk some. But if I'd've been you, I don't reckon I'd've wanted to hear all of it.'

'You heard that too, did you?' Jack said.

'Yeah, I did. You really goin' off to talk to her?'

'After I leave here? What do *you* think?'

Redland considered, gave a small understanding smile in reply. He pushed the door to, but didn't turn the key in the lock of Ralph's cell. 'I'm goin' to leave you here a bit longer, Ralph,' he said. 'You know, tomorrow's another day. It says so, here.'

The prisoner wrapped his arms back around his knees. He turned his head away, spat grimly into the hard-packed floor.

25

SETTING THE TRAP

As they walked back up to street level, Redland handed Jack the pepperbox pistol. 'Take this,' he said. 'It ain't been fired, so it's scarcely evidence. Don't look like it was ever made for shootin' serious.'

Jack grinned. 'But it's a frightenin' thought for someone, if ever it did.'

In the office, there was a man sat waiting for Redland.

'Odd kind of hour to come visitin',' the sheriff remarked testily as Owen Treebucks raised himself from the chair.

'There ain't a regular time for what's botherin' me, Sheriff,' the mine operator said. 'I been thinkin' o' the freight I got stacked with Ormer Pugg. Things bein' the way they are, you should be puttin' a guard at the depot.'

'An' I say, it's a tad soon for me to get that sorted,' Redland rejoined. 'Besides, my argument says it's *your* stock, *you* pay for it.

174

An' for your information, mister, there *is* someone down there.'

'But he ain't,' Treebucks snappily informed the sheriff. 'He took a powder soon as Pugg's body got taken away. The buildin's deserted ... open for almost anythin'.'

'Yeah, I know what you got in mind,' Redland interrupted. 'I'll see to it that someone gets back out there. Meantime, I got places to go, people to see ... startin' up at the Rawlins' house.'

'Who you hopin's there, Sheriff? Miss Rachel ain't,' Parker Meeling said, from just outside the doorway.

'What?' Redland demanded.

The Rawlins' clerk's hands and clothing were blackened by soot from the freight-yard fire. The man's usually clean countenance was darkened by shadowy beard stubble. 'I've just been to the stage office. There was a note on my desk,' he said. 'An' down at the freight yard they said she ordered a hitched team ... got Harvey Maud up to drive her.'

A curse exploded from the lawman. 'Damn her lively hide. Where'd they go?'

'No one said. They headed west.'

'Huh. You say she left a note?'

'Yeah, this here. It's got Harrow's name on

it,' he said, holding his hand out to Jack. Jack thumbed open the fold of paper, read the few penned words.

J. I'll be waiting at Butte –
if you're interested. R.

It was Rachel's writing all right, and for a short moment, Jack's mind went blank. He held back his immediate thoughts, but by the time he looked up a slow crawl of unease was worming its way through his vitals.

'What's it say?' Redland asked, obviously short on temper.

Jack was thinking fast. He was wondering what was going on, how he was meant to respond. Was he supposed to just turn his back on everything, as Rachel appeared to have done? 'She says she's frightened to stay 'cause she knows who shot Pugg. She saw him,' he lied. At that, he folded the note, pushed it into his pocket.

'You goin' to go after her? She say where she's headed?' Wes Humble asked, another town figure who'd joined in with the early morning eagerness.

'I can answer that,' Redland said. 'She's got herself a fat start. So nobody'll be chasin' after her. She'll come back when she gets to thinkin' things out.'

'Why'd you say that?' Humble continued.

'I got her brother banged up. Do you think she'll leave him there to carry the can?'

Jack was thinking that with himself along for safety, that's *exactly* what Rachel Rawlins had in mind.

'Now all o' you clear out. There's other work to be done here,' Redland commanded.

Jack was the first to go, and without even a glance in the direction of the sheriff, hopefully before the lawman could confront him with any lingering suspicions.

Parker Meeling was close behind him as he left the office.

'You think I didn't read that note?' Meeling asked quietly when they were out on the sidewalk. 'What's your game plan now? It ain't such a smart one, is it? Whoever killed Pugg's goin' after Rachel. You've just given him the reason.'

Jack edged his way to the street, let Meeling go on.

'You're usin' her. Like a lamb for slaughter.'

'She *is* if I waste any more time jawin' with you,' Jack hurled back. 'Tell me another way.' Hooked by Meeling's words, he reached for the reins of his gelding. By lying about Rachel's note, he'd exposed her to an unjustified and real danger. But then the message implied more than a shade of guilt. Goddamnit it, he thought, what was done was done, and he'd better get on with it.

When Jack was beyond the darkly deserted Rawlins' house, and the last of the town's outflung buildings, he let his horse out a little. The road dipped sharply across a shadowy, willow-lined stream, and the gelding's hoofs scattered the swift-running water. As they topped the far bank, a man moved away from his horse. He walked slowly from the arching trees and Jack dropped a hand to his Colt.

'You chasin' the stage, or the rider that's followin' it?' Crawford Menroe asked quietly.

Jack held up the gelding. 'It'll be the rider that's followin',' he said, inwardly applauding his judgement, the confirmation of his plan.

Menroe nodded, pointed the carbine he was holding to the ground. 'Well, his tracks are right there.'

'How far ahead's the coach?' Jack asked him.

'A good while. Harvey won't be pushin' his team though. He never does.' Menroe checked his reins, stopped his horse from going down to the stream. 'In this light, he'll be findin' the better road, takin' the coach wide o' the ridge trail. But you don't have to. If you don't take too many chances, you can head 'em off … all of 'em.'

'Why'd I be doin' such a darn hot-headed thing?' Jack asked archly.

'Well, acceptin' they won't all be headin' right back, it's all you got left,' Menroe said plainly. 'So, good luck, feller. It ain't goin' to be an easy ride.' He stepped closer, pushed his carbine into Jack's saddle roll. 'You might have need,' he advised. 'You know, there was a time…

Jack nodded. 'Yeah, I know; you'd've been ridin' point. Thanks, Menroe,' he said, and gave a shrewd smile, waved his goodbye.

The light from early dawn had spread across the mighty sky, was already touching the peaks of the Beaverhead Mountains. Jack heeled the gelding, curious as to why Menroe's hostility towards him had changed. 'That'll be down to Nell,' he muttered, and tugged at the brim of his hat. 'Probably the only reason for ever comin' back.'

26

TURNING BACK

In the smoky, half light of dawn, Jack peered into the wind that stung the knuckle-bruised skin of his face. The coach road ran directly west, and he was taking advantage of its well-worn course. Now and again, he looked for the coach, or the other horseman who was somewhere ahead of him. But they both had some lead, and the fall and rise of the land hampered his vision.

After an hour's steady running, the land became more rugged, started to break against the climb of the rocky draw. It was where the road started the sweeping loop that horse-shoe'd its western end. According to Menroe, it was the route that Harvey Maud took, and Jack agreed with him. He pulled the gelding over as the road swung away. He lifted its head, swung directly toward the ridge proper.

Jack pushed, and for a half-hour, the gelding maintained its gait. The slope of the ridge was riddled with scree, bare save for a scattering of brush and juniper. The ground underfoot was slanted and broken. Jack could feel the horse labouring on the loose rubble that broke from the face of the ridge.

At last he pulled in, dropped quickly from the saddle. 'We'll try an' make it easier,' he said, and taking the looped reins, struck out on foot.

The loose scree shifted and scattered beneath them. By the time they'd struggled halfway up the slope, the pitch rose even steeper. They went up at an angle, quartering the face of the ridge that now only held stunt pine. Deft with its footfalls, the gelding followed at Jack's shoulder. Together they gradually closed on the peak of the rocky draw.

Jack looked down to the west, saw the road where it took on its wide loop. Squinting, adjusting to the light that opened up the land, he could see the coach, the smudge of dust in its silent wake. Three miles distant he judged and, as Meeling said, moving at no great speed. There was no sign of the horseman, and for a while Jack thought he'd got it all wrong, but he hadn't.

At the foot of the ridge, from the shelter of a stubbed juniper, Jack saw the dark shape of a running horse. It was moving away from him, winding a course through the broken scree. The rider was hunched forward in saddle, and Jack watched until they levelled out, set course for the road. Then he turned, was soon back in the saddle looking for the best way down the fronting slope.

They went down, sliding and gouging on braced hoofs with dust puffing high. At the last minute the gelding stumbled, but Jack countered, lifted its head. Then they were on firmer ground and Jack asked the gelding for whatever speed it could gather. But it was already drained, and they made no apparent gain on the rider ahead.

Up ahead, Harvey Maud twisted about. For a long moment, he stared through the dust haze churned up by the wheels. Now, conscious of the horsemen who were fast closing down on the coach, he straightened his back and hauled on the lines.

As the coach slowed, Jack swore. He thought that with Maud's recent experiences, he'd be ever alert, wary of anyone else on the road.

'No, you fool,' he groaned wordlessly. 'She's dead meat if you stop. You an' all, goddamnit. Keep goin'.'

But Jack knew then there was only thing

he could do. He hauled the gelding in, and went fast from the saddle, pulled on the stock of the carbine. He kneeled at the trackside, and levered a cartridge into the chamber. He took a deep breath, exhaled while taking aim, and went for a shot somewhere above and in front of the running horse. He squeezed the trigger, immediately levered in a new round and fired again, then again. Acrid smoke curled into his eye and he blinked against it, saw it was the third bullet that hit the rider.

The other horse still ran on, but the rider had lost control, was reeling in the saddle. He crumpled sideways, lost the stirrups and cartwheeled over the rump of his horse. He hit the ground, made three brutal turns before his body came to rest.

Levering a fourth bullet into the smoking carbine, Jack ran forward, his eyes flitting between the coach up ahead and the man on the ground.

Owen Treebucks' body was sprawled in the dirt. One arm was thrown out crookedly, the fingers grotesquely clawing open air. The other was trapped beneath the stack of the man's inert body.

'You sure caused a lot o' trouble, mister,' Jack rasped. 'Reckon I just about stopped a heap more.'

The mine operator wasn't dead. A dark pool oozed slowly from somewhere beneath him, showed he'd got a low down wound. His eyes were open, were still filled with mean life.

Jack moved closer, stood where Treebucks could see him. 'This'll be the end o' your killin' fling, mister,' he said.

'Damn you, Harrow. How'd you know to get out here? How'd the girl know?'

'She didn't. She never said anythin' about knowin' the names of the killers. I sort o' made that up, a bit like puttin' an eel in a beaver trap.'

'Yeah. But I held down a good enough act. An' we both know Pugg never got to talk. So how'd you know it was *me?*' Treebucks wheezed.

'I thought about it after Hote Stuckley took off with the payroll shipment. Who else knew of it besides me, the Rawlinses an' Parker Meeling? An' Stuckley weren't ever goin' to tell. He thought it would harm his standin', or somethin' equally stupid. You'd think he could've made an exception in your case.'

Treebucks took Jack's explanation in silence. His face twisted into a grimace, was grey and greasy with sweat. 'I never set out to kill anyone,' he groaned.

'Well you did.' Jack turned to the coach as it drew up fifty feet along the road. Rachel was at the window, her face drained of colour.

'He ain't dead ... not quite,' Jack called out. 'If you take him on board, we could get him back to town. But only if you're goin' that way,' he added tellingly.

Without waiting for Rachel's answer, Harvey Maud wrapped the lines around the brake handle and climbed down to help. 'We're all goin' back,' he decided gruffly.

Jack looked back at Treebucks. 'Think you can stand?' he asked.

Treebucks twisted his fingers into the ground and moved one of his legs, choked at Jack's derision.

'The way I look at it, there's laws against aidin' an' abettin' murderers,' Jack sneered. He stepped over to the gelding and pushed the carbine back behind his saddle, turned on his heel when Rachel yelled his name in alarm.

27

LAST SHOT

Treebucks had wrenched free the arm that was pinned beneath his body. In a pain-crazed grip, the Colt's barrel swung up to the level of Jack's chest.

Jack saw the blur of movement, the retained rage in the man's eyes. There was no time for him to pull back the carbine, and at that range a bullet from Treebucks would tear him apart.

He threw himself sideways, jerked the pistol from his jacket pocket as he went down. As he thudded to the ground, the gun in Treebucks' hand blasted, and he felt the sharp pulse of a passing bullet.

Jack levelled the pepperbox and pulled the trigger in the general direction of Treebucks. The detonation was blinding and deafening, as three of the six chambers fired simultaneously.

Jack dropped the gun, stared at the powder burns across his fingers. 'Jeeesus,' he rasped.

He pushed himself to his knees as Maud strolled carefully over to Treebucks, watched despairingly as the coach driver gave the lifeless body a toe-poke.

'*Now* he's got trouble standin',' Maud said with a cold smile.

Jack glanced down at the smouldering pepperbox. '*Someone* was goin' to fire the goddamn thing,' he muttered.

Treebucks' eyes were half closed, rims of white showing beneath wilted lids. The man's Colt had been blasted from his hand, and most of his clothing was now ragged, soaked with the last of his ebbing blood.

Rachel stepped from the coach. 'You weren't comin' to Butte, were you, Jack?' she asked, already knowing the answer.

'I was on the way. But not to indulge you in whatever you got planned, Rachel,' he said.

A few days later, pink light mantled the snow of the distant mountain peaks. Far below, to the east, Jack Harrow was standing in the late sun outside one of his sheds. He was oiling the frame of a bow-saw, while talking to Elmer Redland.

'At least I finally get to know what's goin' on,' the sheriff was saying. 'It seems the

Leesburg owners were wantin' to reopen all them Fishtrap mines. They weren't worked out, just needed proper investment, some new-fangled machinery brought in. Makes for a heap more business.'

'It don't really make sense Rawlins Haulage gettin' burned out then?' Jack questioned.

'Not directly, no. Leesburg wanted to manage *all* the shipments. You know, 'tween the mines an' the town, up to the Butte freight head. But Treebucks elected to misunderstand. He had his own way o' gettin' control.'

'That's tough on Ralph an' Rachel.'

'Was for a short while. But the company's offered 'em a cash settlement ... options too. They said they'd be prepared to buy 'em out proper, or contract 'em, use the vehicles that Ormer Pugg got assembled.' Redland hoisted an approving eyebrow. 'Ralph's learned much recently, says he's goin' to turn a new leaf. Now that would be somethin' risin' from the ashes, eh?'

'Yeah, wouldn't it. Seems like everyone's gettin' to start over. Just possibly, there's somethin' for me here after all,' Jack elected.

'There always was, Jack. You just couldn't see it for a while,' Redland mused. 'Tell me,' he added. 'Hote Stuckley – his crimes weren't ones to die for. Word is, you knew him. So why?'

'Maybe he'd done an' seen enough, Sheriff. I don't know. Me an' him were always goin' to go different ways.'

'Hmm,' Redland uttered thoughtfully. 'Then it's just one more thing,' he said, before wheeling his horse away. 'If you are stayin' – not that's it's any o' my business, you understand – there's a bevy o' young ladies who'll be more'n interested.'

'In what?' Jack asked.

'Whether you're about to do the right thing by one of 'em. What's your current thinkin'?' Redland left the question in mid air while Jack did the thinking.

'Well, now that Rachel Rawlins is so well favoured in business, I'll court her for a day or two, before askin' her to marry me,' he said. 'If she kicks against the idea, I'll maybe settle down with Precious McRae.'

The Sheriff of Laurin Flats shook his head, returned a long-suffering look. 'If I was you, feller, I'd quit your foolin' around an' go for the Yuman girl fast. The way I see it, she could do a hell of a lot better ... *you* couldn't.'

'Yeah, I know it,' Jack said and smiled.

The publishers hope that this book has given you enjoyable reading. Large Print Books are especially designed to be as easy to see and hold as possible. If you wish a complete list of our books please ask at your local library or write directly to:

Dales Large Print Books
Magna House, Long Preston,
Skipton, North Yorkshire.
BD23 4ND

This Large Print Book, for people
who cannot read normal print,
is published under the auspices of

THE ULVERSCROFT FOUNDATION